# CRYSTAL

Anya Finch

# Contents

# Chapter 1

Jane looked in the mirror. She turned her head right, then she turned it left. She didn't like what she saw. Her cheeks were a little bigger than all the ladies dancing around the floor, her chest was not as volumptuous and her skin was pale. It always had been. The only thing she knew she had that the other ladies didn't have was clear, crisp blue eyes. They had the ability to pierce a soul. Her father called her Helen of Troy, he said her eyes could launch a thousand ships. It was a shame her eyes had gotten her no suitors and this was her third season.

She looked in the mirror a moment longer before moving down the hall. There was a record number of people that had attended her father's ball this year and her sister's first season was going far better than anyone in her family had expected. She had danced with nearly every gentleman and she was not at a loss of suitors.

Jane wished she could feel jealous but she only felt thankfulness. Her parents would not lock her in the library and lecture her on how a young lady is to compose herself in the presence of company. She had heard the lecture one too many times.

Her eyes swept over the dance floor. The men looked handsome as they always did, many of them favoring their hair slicked back. The few who went against decorum and let their rugged locks fall about ungraciously atop their heads had to bear accusing eyes from the elderly women in the room all evening. She smiled at herself when she noticed Baroness Claudia put her nose up for a young gentleman who had come to ask her daughters hand for a dance. She held onto her little girls hand a little tighter than usual.

Jane's smile broadened when the gentleman said something and in return received a shriek from the Baroness. Her father's balls never came without incident.

Not wanting to descend and spoil the fun she was having, Jane positioned herself behind a potted plant and continued her watching.

**

Sarah was panting as she returned to her seat by her mother. 'Oh My mama, these gentlemen will be the death of me,' she exclaimed.

'Come now dear you are young and vibrant, a dance here and there surely will not kill you.' Sarah smiled. Her mother, though mature in age, had the soul and spirit of a child. She was just as young as her daughters Sarah's father would say.

'Dear, you have barely danced,' the Duke's voice sounded from the other side of the table.

'Oh papa, have you not seen me? I have danced with every single gentleman in this room. Tall, short, fat, thin, blue, green, and brown eyes. I have seen them all. It is a pity though, not one hold a candle to you papa,' she smiled.

Her father turned his attention to his youngest daughter, 'well perhaps if you were a little older I would have married you.'

'John,' his wife exclaimed, 'the both of you will be the death of me. Where is that sister of yours?'

'Up by the plant mama. You know Jane detests these gatherings. She would rather chew her arm than be down here.'

The Duchess followed the direction of Sarah's pointed finger to see her daughter seeking refuge behind a plant. She sighed to herself. Why her Jane had not the courage of her brother and sister would always be a mystery to her. She was shy and barely spoke unless her brother had said the utter most ridiculous statement against women and their intelligence. Derek knew how to bring her out.

They had had a debate for a good three days about why women are more than just child bearers, not being able to hold his argument anymore, Derek accepted her points and she had smiled at her victory. Jane still spoke of it to date.

Jane moved back when she saw her sister point in her direction. She would definitely receive a lecture from her father when the night was over. She rolled her eyes. They would never understand what it was like to be a wallflower at a ball. All the men would walk by her and ask only the prettiest women for a dance.

She would sit by her mother and the other old women of society. It didn't pass her, their stares and whispers. Humiliation soon takes over. She had made up her mind. This was her last season. She would resign herself to the fact that no man in all of England would find her beautiful and she would die a spinster. An old maid. With cats.

'That is the longest time I have ever seen a woman on her feet without moving,' a voice came out of the shadows.

Jane jumped her hand flat on her chest. 'I am sorry I didn't mean to scare you,' he stepped out of the darkness and smiled. Jane felt her breath leave her. Her eyes widened at the man standing before her. He was the son of a Duke, from a place she could never remember. All the ladies talked about him. His name was, Cedric. His mother, a French nurse, had the fortune of treating her father in a battlefield. Jane slapped herself for not paying attention when her sister would ramble on about this certain man and his family.

'A speechless woman, now that is very uncommon,' he stepped closer, she could hear the French in his accent.

'You must not be from around here, that is exactly what I am referred to,' she closed her mouth. She had found words.

'Well, dear, we shall simply have to remedy that. I am William, Duke of Sussex,' he bowed, 'I assume you are the ever silent Lady Jane, daughter to the Duke of Devonshire?' she nodded. 'It is a pleasure to make your acquaintance,' he lifted her hand and turned it over, kissing her palm.

She felt his hot breath against her skin and it sent shivers down her spine. His mouth stayed hovering over her open hand as his eyes looked straight into hers. He finally released her hand and took a step back and smiled. 'Until we meet again, Lady Jane, it had been my pleasure.' He bowed again and disappeared into the shadows.

Jane stared at her hand like it was not hers. She held it away from her body and looked it over. The heat still fresh on her skin, she looked back to the dancing party below, not a soul had seen what had just happened.

Her sister was happily chatting with her mother and father, none of them had witnessed it. She dropped her hand and smiled to herself and went to back to watching the crowd. Tonight she would have something new to add in her diary.

Tired from standing and watching everyone dance, Jane retreated to her room. She pulled out her diary and sat at her dresser.

Dear Diary, she began.

# Chapter 2

William kept his eyes glued to where Jane stood. He was no longer interested in conversations about horses and women. He had just met the most incredible woman, all of his life he had never seen eyes so blue. They were piercing.

He had noticed Jane when he first walked in she was seated with her mother laughing heartily at a joke he presumed. He had not paid her much attention then. He swept past her bowing to her sister, who was much chattier. Had she said something he would have asked her for a dance.

The night had grown old and he looked around the room to find she was missing. Being a lady, he assumed she had stepped out into the garden with a gentleman for a little privacy. His need to relieve himself overtook his inquisitiveness so he excused himself, and lo and behold, what did he find.

She had not noticed him, her eyes were stuck on the dance floor watching the young ladies turn about in their pretty dresses and the gentleman sway them to the rhythm of the music. He had not meant to speak to her but he felt he would committing quite the injustice to leave her there, letting her know she had gone unseen in her little escapade.

The shock on her face, the widening of her eyes and the way her mouth formed an O when she was startled amazed him. He had seen women of all shapes and sizes and had his fill of them, but there was something about Jane. Her skin was pale and her face was plain.

She was not a strikingly beautiful woman but she wasn't ugly either. Her hair was the shade of a sunset and unlike the other women of the night who had had theirs pinned atop their heads and rained upon with flowers, hers was simple braid tied at the end with a ribbon. This allowed the strands of hair at the front to fall around her face.

She was a goddess.

Her voice when she spoke was soft, not commanding and alluring like the other maidens, but inviting and innocent. He assumed she had a string of suitors vying for her hand but if that was so what was she doing hiding behind a plant.

He watched her behind the plant until he saw her leave. Her mother too had noticed, for she rose up and walked up the stairs. William had to know more about the beautiful Lady Jane, daughter to the Duke of Devonshire.

'Isn't that right William,' his friend Jasper slapped his back, bringing him back to reality.

William simply smiled at the lady standing before him. She was petite he thought to himself then smiled. All women were petite to him. He stood a good six feet tall. She was dressed in red, a very daring color, no doubt a subtle way to inform the men in attendance just what services she could offer them her face was heavily powdered and she spoke while fluttering her lashes.

'William gets a little tongue tied when he sees beautiful women such as yourself Lady...' Jasper let the word linger.

'Maria, Lady Maria, but for friendship you gentlemen could call me Maria,' she smiled at William, what he assumed to be her prize winning smile.

'Well Lady Maria, it is a pleasure to make your acquaintance,' Jasper bowed.

'The pleasure is all mine,' she replied still keeping her eyes on William. All the men had fawned over her yet the one in front of her seemed to be far more interested at staring a plant than having any sort of conversation with her. She was afraid she was losing her touch.

Her mother had not sent for her all the way from Italy to be ignored by the man she was supposed to marry. She prayed her mother had spoken with the Duke and once and for all their life of poverty would end. She had not seen a meal worthy of her station in months.

The little money they had was spent making dresses for her so she would be the belle of the ball. Her father was a fool with no two cents to rub together. He had squandered all their money through gambling. Her mother has pleaded with her parents to provide for them and keep them from sinking into the ground. She had a hefty dowry all thanks to her Italian lineage. Her mother would always say marry an Englishman and you marry a fool. William was the perfect candidate. He was English, he was a man and she had heard about his extravagant lifestyle in France, women being his favorite subject. She fluttered her eyelashes once more, but nothing. His eyes had gone back to the plant.

She curtsied politely and walked away from the gentlemen.

'William, what has gotten into you,' Jasper asked, watching the enchanting Lady Maria walk away. He would have to find her sometime before the night was over for she had something he was greatly in need of.

'All the women here are the same,' he replied satisfied that his darling Jane was not returning.

'My oh my, I never thought I would see the day my darling brother would utter such horrendous words,' Lady Camille spoke from just behind him. His friend would have seen her coming but William's build was far larger than any man he had ever known, his sister looked like a play thing standing next to him.

Jasper smiled and bowed, taking her gloved hand in his and placing a kiss to it. She was the most beautiful woman in the room in his opinion. She was the most beautiful woman that had ever lived. She had poise and cared not for what the ton said. 'Lady Camille.'

'Jasper,' she whispered so no one else heard or a scandal would begin right there and then and she would be whisked off into marriage before she could protest. But marriage to Jasper would not be such a bad thing. 'We have known each other long enough for you to drop those silly formalities. You make me sound like an old maid and I am only one and twenty.'

'You have not lived more than twenty summers Camille,' William said lazily.

She hit his arm and turned red. Jasper knew how old she was. He would have married her when she had her first season, but he respected his friendship with William and William knew his tendencies with women. They both did.

'Tell me was that Lady Maria I just saw. Stay away from her, the both of you. She is nothing but trouble.'

'And how would you know that?' William asked his eyes moving back to the plant, then he saw them. The blue eyes, she had come back. If only she could join the festivities he would be able to talk with her without fear of ruining her.

'Mama says they have no money and her father is set to speak with papa to marry her off to you.'

This caught William's attention. He turned his head to sister so fast he felt his neck snapped. Rubbing the pain with his free hand he squared his eyes at her. It had always gotten her to tell the truth when she was lying.

'I promise it William, it's the truth. The important man you are to meet tomorrow is a Marquis of someplace or the other. Married an Italian woman and squandered all his money. Now they are in debt and he is looking to secure his daughters future. Papa is the richest man in here, it would be a perfect match.'

Jasper laughed. Never in whole life did he see his friend marrying any woman. William had a healthy appetite and a tendency to get bored rather quickly. He never bedded the same woman for than a month, he would not be able to bed the same woman for a lifetime. 'Do not despair dear William, she wore red, surely she has gifts no other woman in here can compete with.'

Camille looked at Jasper with shock. That was his only flaw. He loved women and as long as he loved all other women he would never love her. He saw her as his friend's baby sister. Someone to look after and protect. They never spent much time together but she found him quite handsome with his curly blond hair and sea blue eyes. When he smiled they brightened and his smile was enough to drop any woman at his feet. But William would never approve. He had not approved of the three men who had come to ask for her hand.

He called them wealth diggers, she found the term rather hilarious. Jasper was from a good home. His father was a Marquis and his family had been in business with theirs since the time of their great grand fathers, he was not a wealth digger and he certainly had enough money of his own to give her a good lie. Camille stopped breathing.

A good life? Was she thinking of marriage? Surely not. She wanted to travel to the world before she thought of a man, but how could she? If she did she would return and find him married! Married to the likes of Lady Maria and her wealth digging family!

She was angry and no longer paying attention to the conversation. Jasper would never see her, she stomped her foot and walked away.

'Your sister has quite the ability to rile herself up over things William,' Jasper said as they watched her walk away huffing

William knew why. He knew she had a childish infatuation with Jasper. He had prayed it was a silly young girls fantasy. But the older she got the more intense her stares and flirtatious her conversation became. He turned away three of her suitors away in hopes Jasper would become the man his sister deserved to be with. But there was little hope for change where his friend was concerned.

He had however noticed Jasper tonight. His eyes had followed her through every dance and a hint of jealousy was in his voice when he spoke her dancing partners. William was never one to interfere in a love tale, he hoped they both would find their way to each other but now he had to speak with his father about Lady Maria. He looked back up to the plant and there were no blue eyes, just a green over watered plant and darkness beyond.

# Chapter 3

The Duke watched his son pace his study. William had always been one to listen to reason. The Duke had explained in detail the events leading to a betrothal and asked his opinion. His son's response was a walk in his study. The Duchess watched her son and husband. The two men were so alike. She wondered how a French woman and a British man could sire such a serious person as William. Camille was more of their child than William. She had the carefree nature of her mother and the humor of her father.

The Duchess always teased her husband by saying William had gotten his seriousness from his side of the family, for as long as she lived she had never seen any one of her relatives this serious. He finally stopped and looked at them both.

'Mother, father, I have understood the terms of the betrothal but I cannot accept it.'

'Why not my son?'

'Because Jasper is a friend and I would never subject him to such a fate,' apart from that your daughter is hopelessly in love with the man he thought to himself. Camille would never speak to him again if he allowed it to happen.

'We understand that William but I am not letting any son of mine marry a lady such as Maria,' his mother spoke ever so softly. It reminded him of Jane. She had the same softness in her voice. It was almost a whisper.

'Mother, surely there is a cousin somewhere in want of a beautiful wife. Teddy has always spoken of the joy of organized marriages. And his family is well off. Not of title but well off enough to support an Italian woman's fashion sense.'

'Your cousin Teddy does not favor the women for his relationships William and we both know that,' his father said.

'And he does not want anyone to know, all the better for Maria,' William countered his argument.

The discussed it back and forth until William's father tired of the conversation. He accepted defeat and agreed to speak to his cousin Roswald's and offer Lady Maria to his son. Roswald would be overjoyed. His son was nearing one and thirty and had no woman in his sights. Lady Maria would do well with him.

William left his father's study and wandered about their London home. He found it rather cramped. He was a man of the fields. He lived for the open air and horse riding. When they came to London for the season he only stayed two weeks that was enough time to sample all the women and be done with it.

Jane entered the carriage after her brother. He was a whole foot taller than he had been before he left for school. They had been overjoyed when he returned a month earlier than he had stated. Their mother had thrown a fit scolding him over his choice of travelling with regular people. She had reminded him he was to be a Duke and a Duke behaved in no such way. Sarah and Jane had laughed at the scolding.

They had missed their dear brother so much. 'Tell me Derek where is the beautiful woman you wrote of in your letters?' Jane asked once the carriage began to move.

They were on their way to town to have him fitted for Duke worthy clothes. Their mother had thrown another fit when she looked through his clothes. She swore none of her children were ever leaving her home unless it was to marry.

'She will be arriving in a month.'

Jane's eyes widened, 'You gave her your travel...'

'Ssssh,' he said putting his hand over her mouth. She fought to take it off wondering why he was trying to keep her quiet and it was just the both of them in the carriage. 'Do not speak to anyone about this Jane or I will throw you in the middle of the streets of London and make you talk to every human who walks by you.'

Jane stopped fighting. Her brother knew her well. He knew she feared conversations and people. She kept her mouth shut.

'Mama must never know is that understood,' he looked her straight in the eye to make sure she got his message. Andrew had never had to worry about Jane repeating anything she heard she was far too shy and was far too scared of getting in trouble with anyone. 'Now tell me how was the ball?'

She shrugged, the look from her brother caused her to send a thousand apologies his way. 'It was a ball as all others. The men danced with the women and then the women tried to marry the men,' Derek laughed. Just like his parents he hoped one day his sister would speak to others, not just her family.

She looked out the carriage window and remembered the feeling that filled her whole body when William had kissed her hand. She wished she could see him again but knew it was impossible. He was a man who only talked to beautiful women and they were leaving London on the morrow. Sussex was quite the distance from Devonshire. She had had the best season, her last one.

'Pray tell sister, the smile on your face?' Derek asked

'I am happy to be going back home. I have missed riding. I fear my dear horse has forgotten what it feels like to run in the open.'

He laughed. His sister's love for her horse was the only emotion she ever showed, 'I'm sure he's just fine.' She was the only maiden he knew who rode a stallion.

Her father had bought the horse from one of his many tenants to help him, he had made sure the horse was fed but it was wild. Even their very talented stable hand had had a hard time keeping the horse in line. Jane, however, had worked miracles. It only responded to her. She had talked to it and calmed it down. Since then it had only allowed her and her alone to ride it. She had named it Thunder, because when it ran its hooves shook the ground the way thunder shakes the sky.

They arrived in the town square, mothers and their daughters filled the streets, all of them shopping for the next ball. It was to be held at the Queens palace, her father had been kind enough to exclude his children's names from the list of attendees knowing not one of his three would desire to be in such society.

The carriage came to a stop in front of the shop, Derek helped her out and they walked to the tailors. He tipped his hat at the gentleman that was leaving before giving way to Jane to go in before him. It was rare to see a woman in a man's tailor shop but Jane had the best sense of fashion. Andrew had always turned to her.

'Good day my Lord,' the old man said, 'how may I help?'

'I am here to be fitted for presentable clothing,' he looked at Jane for approval of his words, she nodded. 'I would like three,' he looked at Jane again, she shook her head. He cleared his throat, 'five,' he looked at her again.

'Ten, sir, we would like him to fitted for ten presentable pieces of clothing. You may feel free to add on riding attire as you look around Derek.' She looked from the old man to her brother, both looking at with shock. Jane felt color coming onto her cheeks.

'My Jane, whatever do I need all those clothes for?'

'You have no clothes to wear Derek,' she said in a voice so silent only Derek heard what she said. 'Mama asked me to come with you because you have no clothes. You returned from the America's with rags,' she whispered the last word.

Derek smiled. His sister had courage. She had spoken to him ever so openly in a surrounding that wasn't their home.

'Oh mama please. I approached the foul man at the ball yesterday evening and not even a fraction of his attention was on me. His friend that Lord Jasper was more pleased to have me in their company than that insufferable William,' Maria cried.

Her mother looked out the carriage window. London was bursting with activity during the seasons. It was her favorite time. Her husband had long stopped being the bread winner of the family and Lady Gricella Giovaldi Grant had now taken to lovers to provide her with the finances she needed to run her household. She spotted quite a few gentlemen walking the streets looking bored with their wives.

'You are simply not trying hard enough. If you do not marry wealth Maria, we will have nothing.'

'We have nothing right now mama,' she replied bored with the conversation.

Her mother tapped the top of the carriage and it came to a halt. 'Well you're good for noting father needs presentable clothing for this evenings ball. I shan't be too long,' she said stepping out.

'You will not leave me in this pitiful carriage to be ridiculed mother,' Maria said stepping out after her mother. She had worked herself into a fit. Her mother had put the burden of saving her family on her shoulders. How was she supposed to marry men who wanted nothing to do with her? She was no longer a virgin. Her virtue was ruined. She had thought pleasing a man in bed was a sure way of securing a marriage proposal, how mistaken she was.

The men bedded her and gave her gifts but no proposals came along. She had long since decided she would die a spinster. A poor old spinster.

Maria walked into the shop behind her mother, she looked around and that was when she saw him. The man of her dreams. He was tall, his hair was the right shade of brown it almost looked golden. His beautiful blue eyes were like orbs. Her breath caught in her throat and her heart began to flutter. She looked in the glass window at her reflection.

The man looked past her and smiled at a lady standing by the counter. She turned her head ready to throw snear comments at whoever it was. When she saw the woman, she smiled. She was rather plain. There was nothing memorable about her except those blue crystal eyes. Maria also noticed she looked similar to the man. It must be his sister she thought.

She had not remembered seeing either of them at any balls. She adjusted her dress so her bossom was in clear view of anyone curious to look and walked his way. 'It is quite hot this season is it not?' she asked stopping beside him.

Derek had not noticed the woman come up behind him. He was far too concerned looking through different materials that would fit his mother's approval. Living in the America's had certainly changed him. He smiled at her and nodded in agreement then went back to his task.

Maria pouted and tried again, 'the brown most certainly matches the color of your hair. And if you wear a color so plain, your eyes will very clearly stand out,' she smiled.

'It is hard. My mother insists I have these made. What else does a man need apart from one pair of trousers and a handful of shirts? A special tailcoat for a ball and a pair of agreeable shoes,' he replied with a smile on his face putting in full view a set of perfectly white teeth.

'Well my mother says it is all necessary to catch a wife.'

He drew in a breath and let out a hearty laugh. 'If women choose men for their clothing, they might as well marry our mothers.'

Maria returned his smile. He was quite the agreeable gentleman. She looked about for her mother who was far too busy arguing with old man in the shop. 'I am Lady Maria Giovaldi Grant,' she held out her hand.

Derek looked at her hand wondering why she was holding it out to him. Before he could make a reaction Jane was by his side, nudging him.

'I apologize for my brother. He has lived away for far too long,' she spoke softly.

Maria dropped her hand and smiled, 'It's quite alright. Manners are simply a facade we put on to catch husbands.

Jane smiled and Derek laughed, 'Derek John Weldrake, the next Duke of Devonshire and this is my sister Jane Samantha Weldrake,' he replied.

Maria's eyes opened in shock. Was this the famed future Duke her mother had told her about. All of London was sure he would never return. She smiled her most seductive smile and curtsied, 'My Lord, it is a pleasure to make your acquaintance.'

'Maria,' her mother called her. She quickly said a polite goodbye before following her mother out of the shop. It surely was a good day she smiled to herself.

'I believe you have just caught yourself a wife Derek,' Jane whispered to him. Derek only smiled in amusement. Yes, the lady was beautiful in every way but his heart had already been filled by another. A woman so warm and kind and different from any of the ones he had ever met. He prayed his father would have no objection when she arrived.

Lady Maria gave him one last smile before she left the shop and he smiled back nervously unsure of the look in her eyes.

vote, comment and share..

xoxo....

# Chapter 4



William was beside himself wondering who the man with Jane was. He had cursed himself for having a tinge of jealousy when he saw them leaving the shop and enter a carriage together. Was the young, fair maiden a harlot in hiding? She didn't seem to care they were in the middle of the town and in full view of everyone. Her blue eyes shone with happiness when she looked up at him and he played with her braid like he performed that action every day.

William became frustrated with the thoughts that were causing his temper to come in full view. He had been irritable all afternoon, even when Jasper tried to persuade him a game of cards would quench his foul mood. He was now in the safety of his father's study, alone with his glass of brandy and his thoughts.

That damned woman he had met in the dark hallway had ravaged his thoughts. Her eyes shone like crystals when she smiled, but she was not smiling at him. He had wanted to inquire about her but he did not want to seem too eager, his friend Jasper was an intelligent man and would soon catch on to what was transpiring in William's mind.

He cursed under his breath and poured his whole glass of brandy down his throat in one gulp. It burned him on its way down, William closed his eyes and relished the feeling. What was wrong with him? What was it about this woman that made him so unsettled? He poured himself another glass of brandy and took it down the same way he had the first. He made his decision on the morrow he would call upon her, but first he had to find out where they called home in London. His friend Jasper knew every woman who had come into town for the season, without a doubt he knew Jasper would know where to find her.

'William, shouldn't be asleep?' Camille asked walking into the study. William had always wondered about his sister. She never took caution to female mannerisms, she would walk into rooms without knocking and join conversations with men without a care. She was pretty and quite the intelligent lady but he wondered if she would ever find a man tolerant of her shortcomings.

'Not yet, little sister. Why may I ask aren't you asleep?'

'How can I sleep after the day I have had William?' She dropped herself on the settee. Jasper spent his day gallivanting all over town with you and you both left me here to rot like an old maid. Do you know the conversations mama likes to have? She talks about marriage all day long. I would rather spend time with you and Jasper,' she crossed her arms over her chest.

'You do know Jasper and I spend our time in gentleman's clubs, those are not exactly the places women would be found,' he poured himself another glass of brandy.

'For God's sake William you will drink yourself to a stupor if you don't stop. And I'll have to tell papa, his responsible son has finally joined the rest of London and has become a useless bum. And I will be stuck in mama's company forever!' she raised her hands in the air.

William smiled. The poor girl, she thought the toughest things in life were conversations. She was far luckier than him. Jane crossed his mind again. She seemed so timid at the ball, why then would she be walking about town with a man and laughing like she had no care in the world? William racked his brain trying to find reasons as to why she had seemed so happy. And when the lady in the shop had talked to her companion she didn't seem angered by it. What kind of woman was she?

He knew the legacy of her grandfather and her father, he was a very strict businessman and ran his family the same way he ran his business. How then, was it possible his daughter would risk her reputation and the repu-tation of her family? Did her father know she had a secret lover? He was so lost in thought he did not realize Camille was now standing over him with her hands on her hips.

'William, whatever has gotten you so rattled you better fix it. I refuse to talk to a brick wall. I'm off to bed. I do hope tomorrow you and Jasper will carry me along on your excursions,' her voice peaked when she mentioned Jasper's name.

He watched his sister leave the study. He wondered if Jasper had the same conversations with his brother.

He poured himself another glass of brandy as Jane's smile flashed across his mind.

'Oh Derek,' Sarah playfully hit her brother's arm with her fan. Jane smiled at herself, then felt guilt wash over her. Derek shot her a glare that reminded her she had been sworn to secrecy. If Sarah knew of his fair maiden she would not waste any time, his father would hear of it.

He put the last of their trunks into the carriage before helping his sisters and settling into the carriage himself. He had missed home and enjoyed spending time with his family. They were leaving London for the countryside, which he much preferred. Derek was like his sister Jane, he was rather private and enjoyed the solitude of the countryside. He looked over at Sarah who had already started waving her fan. Soon she would be complaining of the heat and the journey being far too long. She preferred the busy life of the city and the busy men that came along with it.

'I shall fall back into the boredom that has become my life,' she sighed.

The journey back to Devonshire was a tedious one and Sarah's constant complaining did not make the journey any more enjoyable. They made a few stops to eat and drink and rest their horses. When the beautiful manor Jane called home finally came into view, she was silently bursting with joy. Derek looked over at his little sister and smiled. She was a beautiful girl. Much like their mother. Her beauty, however, was not the striking kind like Sarah's, hers was a more secretive beauty. It was a beauty you had to dig down deep to find. Her blue eyes shone in the fading daylight as the carriage came to a stop by the front door. As always the house maids lined up awaiting to welcome their masters back home.

Derek stepped out first then helped his sisters out of the carriage. He took in the beautiful country air. It was truly refreshing unlike London that was filled with far too much women's perfumes and smoke from all the buildings, the streets were far too crowded and the houses were far too close to each other people came calling whenever they felt like it.

Jane looked about her one place where freedom was her right, she smiled to herself. Her library had been alone for far too long.

Sarah stepped out of the carriage with a frown on her face. She had wished they would have stayed on in London. She had just met a fetching gentleman and he had promised to call on her. He would not be able to do that now that she was back to the prison her family liked to call home. 'Oh well, I guess it's back to knitting and watching Cook make the meals,' she commented to no one in particular.

Her mother had learned the art of ignoring her youngest daughter, Sarah could be quite dramatic. She followed her husband inside hoping Sarah would relish the time she still had unmarried and a father who had no more to say than the sheep.

'Your daughter is quite the mouthful Carmen, I wonder, wherever did she catch such a trait?' John teased his wife. He loved all his children equally, he simply had a greater tolerance of Sarah.

'Oh John please do not remind me. The next season is months away what on earth am I supposed to do with that girl. She can't cook, can't knit. All she wants to do is gallivant around the town with men, like those loose women Derek used to speak to.'

'I am quite sure she will settle. Sir Richard's and his very well mannered son requested to call upon us for a month. I believe he will be enough to hold Sarah's attention and we shall pray he does not find her far too overbearing, then we will just have Jane to worry about,' John sighed at his statement. His oldest daughter showed no signs of catching any man's attention. She was far too quiet and when she spoke she was far too opinionated. No man wanted a woman who dared to know more than cook and clean.

# Chapter 5

R emember, vote, like, comment and share...

'Dear me,' Lady Maria waved her fan back and forth with such force, 'this heat is surely going to kill us mother, dare I say.' She rose from her settee and began pacing the room.

'As long as the heat kills you after you have secured a good man who will take care of me,' her mother replied with her eyes glued to the paper in her hand.

'God, mama one might say you do not love me at all. And I may be inclined to agree.'

'Love is for those who have money darling, we have none, therefore no room for love.' She placed the paper on the table before her and picked up another one.

Maria simply looked at her mother. She was so used to her being cold it didn't affect her anymore. She had come to terms with the fact her mother would forever be the kind of person who admired money more than she did human life.

She kept pacing knowing her mother would not even bother to scold her for it. Her thoughts drifted to the shop where she had met the man who she intended to give her all, body and soul. All she had to do was find a way to befriend that sister he was with. She had heard tales of the young Lord Derek. He was as handsome as they come. He was pure perfection. His blue eyes held tales of adventure and kept enough mystery behind them. She wondered what it felt like for his strong arms to lift her onto a horse and carry her down.

The heat in the room seemed to rise the more her thoughts wandered. She looked over at her mother who seemed on the verge of having a coronary. She would mention nothing of her Lord Derek. Her mother would only insist and speak to his parents and if that happened any chances of her securing a romance with him would end. She would keep this man for herself. For her own adventure, for he own pleasure.

'Mama, may I take a walk about town. I'll take Cynthia with me as an escort, she'll be sure to keep me out of trouble,' her mother merely waved in her direction. If there was one thing Maria loved about her mother's love for money, was her complete disregard for what she did.

She called for the carriage to be brought to the front of the house and dragged Cynthia from the kitchen despite her protests and screams. They reached the town, but not soon enough for Maria. She instructed Cynthia to remain in the carriage while she inquired about a dress for her mother from the shop she had met Lord Derek in.

When the door to the shop opened she was disappointed not to find his beautiful face looking up as it did the day before. 'Silly girl,' she said to herself, 'of course he is not here.'

'Miss are you alright?' the shop owner appeared from a door that was kept concealed by drapes of fabric.

'Yes, quite,' she adjusted the bossom area of her dress and the shop owners eyes dropped to her chest. 'I simply wanted to inquire after a dear friend of mine. We were both here yesterday, you may know him, Lord Derek Weldrake.'

'Ah yes miss,' his eyes stayed on her chest a beat longer before they caught hers, 'Lord Weldrake and his family have retired to the country.'

'So soon,' she said ore to herself than to him.

'I'm afraid the Lord Weldrake and his family never stay in London until the end of the season. It's part of their mystery I suppose. We all know so little of them. Their beautiful flower Lady Jane, this will be her last season and her sister Lady Sarah, that one is a beautiful one, her first season out and the town is swarming with rumors of offers on their way after the lass.' Maria smiled. If there was one thing London was good for was its gossip.

'The young Lord Weldrake's return is quite the spectacle especially with the ladies. I assume he's to be married before the end of the year. We all thought he was gone to America's and never coming back.'

'They've retired to Devonshire I presume?'

'Yes miss, the young Lady Jane would have no other way. She dictates how long they stay in London I assume. All she has to say is she is tired of the city and off they go. You could send word of your arrival there miss. I assume they have began planning for their usual ball.'

'Ball?' why would they leave London to host a ball in the country?

'Yes miss, they invite all those who showed interest in their daughters, but I assume it's simply a way for them to continue the festivities of a season in the privacy of their own home. I would do the same thing if I had a manor like theirs.' He ended his sentence with a wink. She smiled her most polite smile and thanked him before exiting the shop.

She would wait for the announcement. If it was a ball they would have to post it. When they did, she would send word her and her mother would be joining their festivity. The thought of seeing the young Lord Weldrake sent shivers down her spine.

'What do you mean they are no longer in London?' William shot up from his chair and he looked more disturbed with the news than he intended. He knew his friend Jasper would not let him breath if he knew about the mystery crystal eyed woman.

'William, if I were not as close as a brother I would say you have finally come to lose your senses. But I know you far better. Tell me why did you ask me to find out if the Weldrake family are still in London. You barely talked to the youngest Lady Weldrake and the older one, well who's to say she is not a myth.' He dropped onto the settee in the most ungentlemanly manner, 'Oh do not tell me William, you are like the men we whisper about in the club?'

William threw a piece of crumpled paper at him. Jasper was a good friend but his life was a torrent of women and no sign of commitment in his future, near or far. He felt for his sister she would forever be holding out hope for him.

'I simply had business I wanted to discuss with Lord Weldrake. My father plants cotton and I heard rumors Lord Weldrake was looking to expand his fortunes outside what he currently does.'

'Yes,' Jasper pretended to believe his story, 'which is?'

'I do not have details Jasper, I'll have to ask my father,' he paused then quickly added, 'it was his idea.'

Jasper waited to be sure his dear old friend was finished with his lie then held a thoughtful look before bursting out in laughter. 'William dear brother, we both know that is not the reason you look like someone who's about to die, but I shall pretend I believe you. Where is you dear sister today?' he swiftly changed the subject.

One of the benefits of having William as a friend was his beautiful, but too young sister. She was everything he wanted in a woman but his friendship to William would ride the line if he decided to pursue his feeling further.

She had looked lovely at the ball, he regretted not snatching her away in a corner and making her blush like she always did. He wondered about the man she would marry, whether he would be good to her be like all the other men who married simply to have a wife and please their mothers. She always spoke of love. She wanted to marry for love and so did he but he had come to learn love and marriage did not go hand in hand.

He shook away the thoughts, what was he thinking of marriage for? He was still miles away from marriage and the women in London were not falling into short supply anytime soon. Camille's face flashed across his mind again. She was beautiful.

'Which one of us has something to hide now, Jasper?' William's voice cut through his thoughts. 'My sister is away somewhere fawning over some gentleman who had the insanity to send a letter. She has not stopped speaking of it.'

'Yes, well, a young beautiful lady like her, she must have a million men want to fall at her feet,' he said with a tint of sadness in his voice.

William held back his chuckle. His friend was as transparent as the day was warm. Just then the door opened and in came Camille with a piece of paper in her hand, Jasper did the gentleman thing and stood up. She held up her hand, 'please Jasper, we are at home, sit back down I am not the queen,' she closed the door behind her.

'Camille if mother sees you running about the house this way,'

'Oh God, William, you are more of a bore than she is.'

'What's that you've got there? A suitor, no doubt?' Jasper said in an uninterested voice. He was coming to realize how annoyed he was by the mere fact William had not been lying to him,

She looked over to him, really seeing him for the first time since entering into the room. William sat back down, he had seen this happen before. Camille looked over Jasper in his well tailored shirt and coat. He was always one to brag about his sportsmanship all through his university years and it showed in the muscles in his legs, and that is where his dear sister's eyes landed. She looked him over so shamelessly William began feeling embarrassed for her.

Jasper not even noticing his deepest privacy was being invaded kept his eyes glued to a book laying beside him.

'Camille,' William spoke with authority,' his sister jumped a good foot away from the spot she was standing in.

'Papa wanted me to give you this,' she walked over to him making sure to use the route furthest away from Jasper. 'It's an invitation to Devonshire, Lord Weldrake is throwing his annual after season ball,' she rolled her eyes. She never quite understood why one would leave London a week before the end of the season and then throw a ball on the very same day the grand ball happened in London. She had always found that family quite queer.

Their eldest daughter especially, she hardly spoke and when she did it was with a few words at most. Now that they had received an invitation they would have to go. She hoped Jasper and his family had not received one, she was looking forward to trying to see real men in other people the way she saw a real man in Jasper. 'Excuse me,' and she ran from the room like she was being chased.

Jasper stared at the door a long while after she had gone. What was it Camille always ran from in his presence? She would enter the room in a jovial mood and by the time she was leaving she looked almost terrified. He turned his attention back to William who was choking the invitation in his hand to death.

'I guess my questions about town are to come to a stop.' William shot him a look that he very well understood. Jasper stood up, bowed and took his leave

# Chapter 6

E xtra lengthy,,,,for you my readers,...

Lady Weldrake was fussing over their ball, as she did every year. Sarah had made a wise choice and made herself scarce under the pretense of finally wanting to learn how to cook. Her mother, oblivious to her new found interest, was pleased she had finally taken interest in the works of running a household. Jane was not as lucky as her sister. Her mother had cornered her after breakfast, knowing full well her eldest daughter would not be in attendance.

'Jane,' her mother scolded. She was simply seated by the window looking out into the garden. 'If you will not attend the ball at least pretend to be interested in making sure your home looks glamorous and inviting.'

Jane rose slowly and came to stand next to her mother who now seemed more satisfied. They spent the whole afternoon looking over patterns, colors, menus and sniffing candles. By the evening Jane was sure she had a headache from all the scents she had inhaled. She had retired to her room immediately after supper under the guise of a headache when all she wanted was to sit in silence and hope William and his family would attend.

She had seen the invitations that had been sent out and his family name had been at the top of the list. From what she was able to gather from old gossip in the kitchen William was a man who had taken his pleasures very openly with his long time friend Jasper. A certain Lady Maria was trying to marry him and he was a silent rake but a rake all the same. She reminisced their conversation at the ball and smiled as she lifted her hand and looked at it like it as not her own.

'You are being far too silly Jane,' she reprimanded herself as she dropped her hand. She was far too shy to be seen by anyone and the first man that accosted her would win her heart, isn't that what shallow debutants did. Fell over themselves in fantasies that did not exist. She believed in love, her mother and father had it. She had seen them steal kisses in the hallways when they thought no one was there. She watched how her father kept an eye on his wife when they were tending to their duties in ballrooms, he watched her like a hawk.

She smiled to herself as a memory came to her of her father nearly challenging his own brother to duel because her mother had paid him far too much attention during his visit. Her father was ready to turn his own brother away because of it. Her dear Uncle had not visited since, he simply inquired about their wellbeing through letters.

A knock on the door interrupted her thoughts, Derek walked in without waiting for her to answer. He closed the door behind him and stared her down. She loved her brother but sometimes she wished he would just leave her be. He was the only one in the house that was ever insistent she come out of the shadows. The rest of her family had accepted her as she was and hardly pushed but Derek was far too insistent it sometimes angered her.

'I do thank the good Lord he made me a man, if I had to endure half of what you and dear Sarah go through, I would be in a grave by now.'

'Derek, for the love of,' she stopped. Their household was not often in church but she knew not to use the Lord's name in vain. 'Why would you say such a thing? Your visit to the America's surely stripped you of any manners papa instilled in you.'

Derek laughed at her reprimand. He placed himself on the bed next to his sister. If only the society knew his sister. She would make an excellent wife. She was humorous beyond anything and she had a fire in her eyes when they argued. She read more than any other he knew and that made her intelligent. He understood, to an extent, as to why she feared being in the middle of a social event, her inability to stand by and watch her kind "women" being discussed like they were chicken being traded would surely disqualify her from any marriage mart. She was the reason he had given his heart to a woman who had an opinion of her own and voice to make her opinion known. He admired his sister more than he cared to let her know.

'I have lost none of my manners Jane, a gentleman is still a gentleman even if he is resides elsewhere.'

'Is that so? The lady in shop the other day would highly disagree. Have you truly been gone so long you have forgotten simple decorum Derek? I simply must ask how you treat your lady love, is common respect has escaped you.' She looked him straight in the eye. They both inherited their mothers blue eyes, unlike Sarah who took after their father. Her eyes were honey brown.

'I did not miss your never ending scrutiny while I was away. But if you must know our friends across the ocean do not pay as much heed to "decorum" as you put it. The men know how to respect women but we do not stand at arm's length until the wedding night,' this earned him a glare from Jane. Her eyes had the ability to turn so icy when she was upset or when someone said something like what he had just said.

He smiled and placed his hand on hers, 'You do not have to worry I have not forgotten everything that father taught me. If she has been compromised I promise it is not by me.'

Jane sat back letting her back rest on the board of her bed. She looked at Derek. He was speaking like one who had lost his mind. She had heard of tales of men who went mad once returning to England after years away, the society was too much for them after experiencing freedom. Her brother certainly sounded like someone who had finally lost his senses. 'You mean to tell me you would marry her even if she was not pure.'

'I would be the only one who would know Jane, it would not matter to me, as long as she loves me and I her, I do not see what difference her purity makes.'

Derek John Weldrake,' Jane shrieked. 'You have completely lost your sense. I pray mama does not hear the ridiculous things coming from your mouth. Is this what you were doing while you were away? Becoming a rake like all the other men in our society with little to no regard to a woman or her body and only looking out for your own wants and needs.'

Derek laughed. His sister was truly unmatched. The man who would marry her had a lifetime of theatrics to look forward to. He had missed her dearly. 'Relax sister,' he said between laughs. 'I am as pure as the day I was born I promise you,' he held up his hand, 'and so is my beloved. yes it is true they do not take purity as seriously there as they do here, but I was raised by a man and where he failed you made up for in scolding. Your children will have hell to pay when they cause you trouble,' he smiled.

Jane relaxed. Derek's sense of humor had never been amusing to her. He vexed her in the most unsuspecting ways. She was glad he had not turned into men like William. 'I came to wish you a good night and to remind you about your promise. I returned unharmed, you owe me a dance little sister,' he kissed her head and walked out leaving her no room to argue with him.

'The ball is upon us,' Sarah exclaimed as she walked into her dear sister's room. Jane was seated by the mirror staring at herself. Tonight she would have to go down, she would have to dance, she would have to talk. She felt numb. Sarah seemed far too excited. She had had a good season opening. All the men who hoped to have her as their wife were sure to attend. No one would take a second to look in Jane's direction.

In London she could hide, but not at home. Her father was far stricter on her appearances when they retired to Devonshire.

'Come now Jane,' Sarah said pulling her from the chair. 'You look like a vision and guess what, Lord Cartwright and his family are in attendance and so I the Marquis of Sunderland's son, Lord Jasper Wieldon, can you imagine.

There is also a rather ravishing lady with her bossom a little too exposed for mama's liking, she has been liking about her since she arrived. Charlotte and Margaret are here too and Charlottes older brother. He has grown into quite the young man. He looks stunning,' Sarah noticed her sister seemed un moved by her introductions to the guests, 'his name is Lord Matthew. He just returned from Spain.'

'I wish I cared for these people as you do Sarah, but I would rather...'

'Sit in your library and fight with Derek over which sex is smarter, I know,' she said rolling her eyes. 'But you promised if Derek returned home safe and sound, which he has, you would dance with him and attend the ball after the dance. But I have news that will blow your skirts away.'

Jane gave her sister a murderous look. She wondered where her siblings found the blunt language that rolled off their tongues. 'Sarah, who will marry a man who speaks so freely as yourself. You will send these poor men running, looking for proper wives.'

'Oh please Jane, we are locked in a room that no one would dare enter. Apart from you, no one ever hears me speak like this. Anyway, Lord Cartwright has kept guard by the staircase, mama says he is waiting for us to descend.'

Jane felt warm. The hand he had kissed began to tingle. She turned back to the mirror with the pretense of making sure her hair was in order to escape the ever noticing eyes of Sarah Weldrake. She took a deep breath,

Sarah took hold of her hand and pulled her to the door, 'well then, we shan't keep the Duke in waiting any longer.' Jane took her sisters hand and prayed for the best.

Derek was waiting for his sisters at the top of the staircase. He never quite understood why it took ladies twice the amount of time to prepare for a dance they looked rather beaten afterward. He had donned one to the coats and breeches he had purchased in London under Jane's watchful eye.

'My oh my, dear brother, dare I say you will take the Italian lady's breath away dressed like that,' Sarah said as she and Jane emerged.

Derek was left shocked. His usually reserved sister had on a dress that was far too daring for the reputation she had built herself. It was a beautiful lavender with lace on the top covering her shoulders but revealing them at the same time. From the waist it flowed and danced around her feet playing with the notion of kissing the ground. Her hair was held in its usual braid safe for the blue ribbons added to it that made her look almost mythical. Her cheeks were a shade of pink, he assumed from embarrassment and her lips had a tinge of red. Sarah had done well

'I will be dancing with the most beautiful girl in the ball tonight Lady Jane,' he said as he kissed her hand. Sarah cleared her throat, 'the two most beautiful girls,' he corrected. He took each of their hands and led them down the stairs.

When they reached the bottom, the footman announced them bringing the crowd to a standstill. William's attention was quickly drawn from his conversation with Jasper to the staircase he had temporarily left. He silently cursed himself inside for abandoning his post.

He had not expected Jane to make an appearance. She looked lovely in her lavender gown that complimented her in the best way.

'I must say William, I now know the reason for all those inquiries,' Jasper said into his ear.

The night went by, William kept his position watching Jane dance the night away with her brother. He was the only man she had shared the dance floor with.

'Come now brother,' Camille said as she came to stand by him, 'why not ask the lovely lady to dance instead of standing here looking rather suspicious. I have already heard those old haggard spinsters questioning your presence here.'

He looked at his sister. She had a great point, as always. Ever since that night he had not been able to stop thinking of her and her crystal ball eyes. He wondered how conversations with her would go, what it felt like to see her smile and hear her laughter. He wondered if she could sing or play the piano. Did she enjoy riding? Those questions would not be answered if he kept standing and staring. He finished the drink in his hand with one gulp and handed the glass to Camille. 'You are far wiser than your age.'

'Yes, if only the gentlemen in attendance tonight wanted a woman for her brain instead of her body,' her eyes travelled to where jasper was standing with a red haired beauty. He had just said something funny and she tilted her head back and let out a rather seductive laugh. She let out a sigh. William watched his sister and smiled, he wanted to help but tonight he would need to help himself first. \he stalked over to where Jane was sitting.

She was alone and the song playing was close to the end, the next dance was the waltz. He had had many a waltz's with intentions far from proper, but tonight all he wanted to do was dance.

'Excuse me, Lady Jane, we meet again,' he bowed and held out his hand for her. She looked up a little startled. She immediately looked around the room, he assumed looking for her brother. 'May I have the next dance?' he asked

'Of course you may,' a voice from behind him came. 'Jane adores the waltz and she dances it with the grace of an angel, don't you Janie?' her brother smiled. William noticed an exchange between the two siblings. He was the one who knew Jane well. It would be profitable to propose to his father the business he was thinking of, that would indefinitely that would require him to spend ample time in Devonshire.

Jane looked between her brother and Lord William. She regretted ever agreeing to Derek's stupid plan. She knew he would return safe and sound.

She rose from her seat and put her hand in Williams and let her lead him to the dance floor, but not before giving John her most unamused look. He would pay for doing this to her. They positioned themselves and waited for the music to start playing. The violin went first and his hand found its way to her back, the other taking a firm hold of hers. His strength was impressive.

The felt flutters in her stomach as he took the first step and pulled her body to follow. It was not a forceful pull, but one that felt like an invitation to follow him on a journey. She followed his steps with ease and fear at the same time. As they turned his hand left her back and she felt empty, but only for a moment because it placed itself back this time guiding her in a circle. Then, the music made a dramatic pause. William stood his ground, holding her hand with a force that assured her he would be there always. She took that moment to look in his eyes. She had kept her eyes to his shoulder for his height did not allow her to look straight into his eyes. She found the most beautiful golden orbs looking down at her. They held a smile in them, like they had a secret between them that they shared. 'It is a pleasure to make your acquaintance again Lady Jane,' he said

'The pleasure is all mine, Lord William,' she wanted to look away but he held her gaze. He looked at her so intently she feared she may scream for lack of any other reaction.

The music began again and she let out a sigh of relief. He guided her through to end of the song. 'May I offer to get you a refreshment, Lady Jane?' he asked not letting go of her hand. He led her to the refreshment table.

'I was not expecting you down here tonight Lady Jane.'

'Neither was I Lord William,' she replied accepting the glass from him. Their fingers brushed each other and that same spark of electricity she had felt came again.

'I shall ask you for one too many things tonight Lady Jane as I do not know when I will have the pleasure of seeing you again.' She gave him a questioning look. 'A small conversation perhaps, in view of your father of course, I already see your brother looking about for you.' She turned to find Derek looking over the crowd.

'I do not bite Lady Jane, despite what my reputation may have implied,' he received a smile from her. So she had heard of him. His past was a ghost that had proven to haunt him.

'A small one, I must retire soon.'

'Do you have some place to be tomorrow?'

She squinted her eyes a little, 'I do not mean to be rude, but that is no concern of yours Lord William.'

He was taken aback by her bluntness. His mother had always said the quiet ones were the ones to look out for. 'I apologize for my lack of discretion Lady Jane, I am usually not this forward.'

'I certainly hope not, Lord William,' her eyes were now fiery. Jane was not the one to speak but she did not entertain rudeness from anyone. Her parents had schooled her on proper conversations and she was well aware the man before her was far from proper. He was used to talking to loose women who would gladly do what he asked of them, if only to say they are 'close friends' of the Duke in waiting.

'I do hope I have not wavered any interest you had shown in my direction,' his eyes holding her to where she was standing. William was an attractive man, who stood at an attractive height.

'And... who said I hold any interest in you Lord William? Your reputation has clearly misled you. Not every unmarried woman seeks the company of a man.'

He now fully turned so he was facing her and not the overbearing crowd of English society, 'is that so Lady Jane, please do tell, are you one of those women?'

'The kind of woman I am is not the current topic of discussion Lord William,'

William was stunned. She was educated. It showed in her speech. She was not like the other women of society whose expanse of knowledge was fashion and gossip. If he was right, judging from her choice of clothing, she was not overly influenced by fashion. If he was to pick the best dressed woman in the room, it would not be the woman standing next to him. But yet, she was the one who shone the most. Her quiet and timid demeanor was simply a mask to hide the well bred and well read woman she was inside.

She had an opinion, one he wanted to know. 'You are right Lady Jane, it is not, but I would like to know what kind of woman you are,' his eyes shone with anticipation. He knew she would not answer his question this very night, but she would answer it.

Before she had a chance to respond, Lady Maria had placed herself by his side. Jane held back any response she was about to give. She eyes the woman beside him and remembered her from the shop. She was the woman who had spoken with her brother at the shop in London.

'Lord William,' she gave a low bow, 'I never thought I would see attend a ball in the country, this your first one I presume?' she asked but she kept her eyes on Jane.

'Yes it is,' his eyes firmly on Jane as well.

All she could do was look between the both of them. She wanted to excuse herself and give the pair their privacy, silently laughing at herself for thinking William was the kind of man that would give her an audience because he found her... her thoughts were interrupted by her brother's hand. He linked his arm with hers as he planted himself by her side, more to keep her there than join in on the conversation.

Maria smiled to herself, not exactly like she had planned but she knew Jane was her key to the future Duke. Her mother would be rather pleased with her. Standing in the company of two future Dukes. She bowed to Derek and he acknowledged her presence with a nod of his head.

'Lady Maria,' she said, 'we made our first acquaintance in London. I see the tailor did you well, she complimented his tailcoat.

'Thank you, would you care to dance?' Derek asked

'I'm afraid I do not have a dance card, my Lord.'

'Please, my father is my Lord, you call me Lord Derek.,' he held out his hand to her and began leading her away from Jane and William dismissing the need of a dance card in his own home.

'Where were we?' William asked once they were alone once again.

'I was bidding you a farewell. Thank you for the refreshment Lord William,' she said handing him back the glass. 'I must retire now,' with that she gave a short curtsey and disappeared through the forming crowd.

William was left dumbfounded. She was as timid as she appeared on their first meeting. Now he only wanted to know her more.

# Chapter 7



Read, like, share, comment

Jane retired to the comfort of her room. She had had enough excitement for one night. The dancing had been fun. The dancing with William. He was a man of strength. The way his hand commanded her body and pulled her like she weighed the same as a feather. She still felt the imprint of his hand on her back and the warmth of it on her palm.

She could hear his voice in her head, his French accent rolling off his tongue, like a light wave turning about on the sea. His eyes were so brown they became golden in a lit room. She stopped herself before her thoughts carried her any further. He was Lord William, all he wanted was a woman to pass his time with. She would be traded in a week. But that did not stop the rushing feeling inside her. She felt like a child again. So fresh and so new.

She heard a soft knock on her door then the voice of her ever insistent brother before he turned the handle and opened it. His head emerged first, when he saw she was still awake he let himself in. 'A rather eventful evening was it not?' he as ked as he placed himself on her bed.

'Not as eventful as Sarah would appreciate,' she replied dryly not wanting to divulge her true feelings.

'You left too soon, there was a brawl right in front of mama and papa. Two men fighting for our dear sisters hand. She let them know right there and then she would not marry a man who dared raise a fist. None of them were given a chance to defend themselves.'

Jane laughed. It had been Sarah's dream to have men fight for her, now that it happened her dear sister must have felt ever so important and wanted. And it was just her first season. She would surely enjoy London next year when the soldiers attended the season.

'But tell me, Lord William kept you rather occupied. What could you both have to say to each other? He talked to no one else after you left he kept his post by the refreshment table, serving young women. Mama even asked if someone had hired him.'

'He was simply making polite conversation with the host of a ball, there is nothing to it Derek. You have always been one to see smoke where there is no fire.'

'Correction my dear sister, I see the smoke before the fire.'

'Yes, Derek, whatever you say. May I sleep, you tired me tonight,' she said not waiting for his permission to enter into her bed. She pulled the covers over her and turned to him. 'When is your love arriving? I would very much like to meet the woman who has stolen my brother's heart.'

'In a week.'

'You seem worried. She may share my bed if you are worried there is nowhere for to sleep,' Derek smiled.

'It is our father I am worried about,' Derek never said father, unless he was worried or scared. Jane guessed he was scared. Their father was a liberal man, but he valued family and was always vocal about his desire to see the title fall to his son and a beautiful English woman who knew the value of the title Duchess.

'Papa is not so unkind as not take into consideration your happiness. We have heard his story a thousand times. His father was against his marriage and he was able to make grand papa see reason. I do not see a reason why you should be worried.'

'You are far too wise, I wish Sarah would have some of your intelligence.'

'Do not speak that way of your sister Derek or I shall be the one opposed to your union. Sarah is young.'

'As were you.' He kissed her forehead not wanting to continue the conversation any further. He left her room with doubts still running in his mind. If Jane was right, he would be married by the end of the year.

Jane was seated in the garden with a book in her lap but her attention was far away. In a past that seemed so distant. She had not slept, William invaded her thoughts the whole night. She had seen them dance over and over again. She had felt his hand in hers, she had seen his eyes looking into hers. He seemed like he was holding onto her every word, afraid they would stop coming. Even now awake she was not able to rid herself of thoughts of him. It was a warm day and Jane suddenly felt the need to feel the rush of air around her.

It was still early and a horse ride before lunch was exactly what she needed. She closed the book and rose with the intention to go riding as she was. She stopped when she was the tall figure walking towards her. Her breath caught in her throat. William.

His hair a little messy a top his head was being swayed a little by the light summer breeze. Jane felt the need to disappear behind the nearest rose bush, but he had already seen her. He slowed a little before continuing on his path. Jane looked to the house and saw Derek by the door leading to the garden.

'Good Morning, Lady Jane,' Sir William reached her before anymore thoughts could develop in her head. He bowed and took her hand before she offered it and turned it over. He placed a kiss on her palm and let his mouth linger over her soft skin. She felt like she had just been struck by lightning. Her whole body tingled from the point his breath was hovering over to her toes.

Jane pulled hand away like she had been charged with electricity. 'Lord William,' she said a little more unamused than she intended.

'I apologize for calling upon you this way...,'

'You apologize a lot for someone who does not at all feel sorry for his actions,' she interrupted. William was taken aback by her words, again. As was she. 'It is my turn to apologize,' she added quickly. Jane felt the need for a savior at that moment. But she knew Derek had offered strict instructions for them not to be disturbed.

'A small walk shall remedy any offence I may have taken from your statement,' he positioned his hand to receive hers.'

She looked at him questioningly before placing her hand neatly in his. Jane needed not worry about being chaperoned, her mother never encouraged it for her. Jane sometimes thought her parents would be glad if she was compromised, if only to ensure she got married.

'It is a warm day, had I anticipated it, I would have arrived in my riding habits.'

Jane looked up at him, but the sun blocked his face from her complete view. He was a handsome man. His chin held light hairs, just like her father. He never shaved clean. His lips were welcoming enough, she looked away, ashamed of the direction of her thoughts.

'Do you ride Lady Jane?'

'Sometimes, when the weather permits.' They continued walking in silence. William took her silence as a sign of lack of experience where conversation was concerned. This was the quietest walk William had ever been on. The conversations during his walks usually centered around flirtations and promises of rendezvous later in the evenings. But with Jane, he doubted such topics would appease her. He wished he knew, perhaps, an interest of hers, something that would open a door for him into her world.

'I don't suppose you have an interest in books?'

She smiled, 'yes I do actually.'

'Is there a particular book you hold high esteem for? Perhaps romance?'

She turned her head to look at him, he was much taller than her and she had to tilt her head back, 'I am not one of those girls running about dreaming of a man on a horse that'll come and save her. I enjoy educational reading. We live in a society that does afford the same opportunities to women that it does with men, so our education is limited to a governess.'

'And your governess, was uneducated?'

'She cared more for the men in our household than in imparting any kind of education in us. As you can clearly see in my sister Sarah. She dreams of a life that is non-existent, she dreams of men riding on horses and a love...' she stopped. Jane was sure with her opinions William would not be returning, but then he stopped and turned toward her.

'A love? So you do not believe in love?' she was beautiful and she did not have a clue. Her skin was pale in the sunshine, which told him she spent many hours locked in her father's study or a library. Her blue eyes almost seemed gray now that they were in the sunlight and her hair shone as the light rays washed across it. He wished in this moment to take her to Gretna Green and be done with the process.

'I have no opinion of it Lord William,'

He coiled. He had scared her with such a direct question. 'Do you wish to return?' She simply nodded her head. This was going to be harder than William thought. She was lovely but not as open as his other willing explorations. He turned and waited for her to place her hand in his before walking back towards the garden he had found her sitting in. how would he be able to conquer her heart if she was so afraid to be who she really was? 'May I ask one last question, Lady Jane?'

She nodded. 'Why are you so timid?' she stopped walking and removed her hand form the warmth of his.

'I do apologize I am not as whorish as your usual escapades Lord William, but I was raised on morals. And as to my silence, what could you and I possibly have in common to speak of?' with that she walked ahead of him, at a pace that was certainly unladylike as she had to lift her skirts slightly to keep from falling.

William was again left dumbfounded. She was a character for sure. For a woman so shy and withdrawn she certainly had strength. He assumed her brother was the reason for it. He would return again, and try to win her over another way, but first he needed to attend to past business.

5

# Chapter 8

'They were simply expressing their interest in me papa, surely you will not have them sent to a prison for wanting to wed your daughter?' Sarah was beside herself in her parents room. She had sang on and on about the two men who had taken to fists to prove which one was worthy.

'Yes Sarah, I have heard you, but if they were willing to fight each other to prove a point who's to say he will not take to fists when you have a disagreement?'

'Uurgh,' Sarah said as she lifted her hands in the air. According to her, her parents were being unreasonable. She did not see what was so serious about men being men. They were both rather handsome and they both came from a wealthy family. 'If anything papa, you should be glad you have a daughter that would inspire such passion,' she said with her hands on her hips. To her this was her way of standing her ground. She would not let herself be bored in the country until a new year came round for them to leave for London again.

The ever so handsome Wilkshire had offered to call on her and her father had adamantly refused to receive him. 'Yes, well Sarah you do remember your aunt. She is long cold in the grave but do not forget what took her there.'

Sarah rolled her eyes. Her mother had told her this story far too often. Her famous Aunt Agatha had had the misfortune of marrying a man she did not know had an addiction to the bottle. Because of this addiction he turned to violence on occasion and one day he pushed Aunt Agatha down the stairway and she did not wake up.

From then on Lord John Anthony Weldrake had sworn to never let a man who seemed to have a love for more than gentry manners and balls. 'I will not be the one to send you off to your undoing Sarah and that is that. We are no longer having this discussion.'

'You want me to die a spinster at the age of a hundred and five papa,' she screeched.

'I want you to leave this earth at the age of a hundred and not now,' her father replied. She stamped her foot and left his study. Lord Weldrake had a lot to learn from his wife. Carmen could listen to Sarah complain all day and still have a calm demeanor about her. He had already lost his patience and if she had continued protesting he would have sent her to stay with wife's cousin on their farm in Northern Scotland.

Sarah slammed Jane's bedroom door. Jane looked up from her book in shock, what an entrance sister.'

Sarah dumped herself on the bed, 'papa is not going to let Wilkshire escort me in any manner, he wants me to be alone for the rest of my life,' she sat up, 'how on earth does he expect me to make a match when he wants to keep me locked in here with no man visiting me?'

Jane took a deep breath. Derek had made himself scarce since his return. He always chose to leave their father's managers and go check on the tenants.

'Sarah, this is your first season. It is hardly the time to be taking things this seriously. And I must say I agree with pap on this, Aunt Agatha...'

'Yes, Janie, I know, she married a man addicted to the bottle and he beat her and pushed her down the stairway. We have all heard this story.'

'And because you know it so well, you know what it did to papa and that was his sister who had decided we were not good enough family. Imagine what it would put him through if it happened to his daughter?'

Sarah was frustrated why did no one in this household see her point. She did not want to spend her days knitting and cooking and learning how to fold sheets and reading. She wanted to go riding and be compromised next to the stream. She wanted to have an adventure. She wanted to escape her life. 'Charlotte has already been kissed Jane. Can you imagine. She explained it to me and it sound like pure joy.'

'Sarah!' Jane exclaimed. Lady Charlotte was well in her way to becoming one of the women who wore red at balls. She had been compromised by almost all the men in London and she was still the tender age of one and seven. 'And that is an example you want to live by?'

'Why not? Don't harlots have more fun than the rest of us?' this earned a squeal from Jane.

'Goodness gracious Sarah, if mama heard you, you would not leave the four walls of your bedroom.'

'Oh please Janie, you want to tell me you have never wondered what it feels like. All those books you read, it has never crossed your mind? And you have the perfect opportunity to try, Lord William has taken quite the interest in you. And mama does not require you to have a chaperone.'

Before Jane could answer, her door opened again and this time her brother walked in looking rather distraught. When he saw Sarah on her bed, he reformed his expression. Jane looked at her two siblings and wondered why her door was always the one to be opened when they had troubles. Sarah stood up knowing Derek preferred talking to Jane rather than her. It didn't bother her, he always wanted to be so serious and often was just a softer voice of her fathers. 'Think about what I said Janie,' she said as she stood up. She gave Derek a kiss on the cheek before disappearing and closing the door behind her.

'And what do you have to think about?' Derek asked. He knew Sarah was up to no good. Always trying to make Jane be as eccentric as she was.

'Marrying. What's wrong?' she quickly changed the subject.

'Sarah wants to marry?'

'Sarah wants many things Derek, I can hardly keep up with her wants and needs. Now tell me what is that look on your face?'

'It's Leila, she is arriving tomorrow.' Jane looked confused. 'My fiancée.'

'Derek, you never mentioned you were engaged to be married.'

'No I did not, because it is not of importance.'

'Yes it is Derek, an engagement is a promise to marriage. You are practically married to her.'

'No I am not, I am engaged. Words are used differently in America.'

'Yes, but you are now in England. How do you plan to explain this to papa. He surely will kill you.'

Derek was not expecting this reaction. He had wanted to tell her the night they had spoken but she looked so tired he did not want to give her sleepless nights. But it seems he should have spoken to her that night because now she was being far too judgmental. 'Jane you must understand, she is the one for me. I have seen and spoken with the beautiful English debutantes and they squirm and throw tantrums like Sarah. Do you think I enjoy that. You of all people know. Do you honestly think I enjoy talking to empty women who have but one goal, to capture a husband.' His voice was now strained. He wanted Jane to see his point and to side with him, so when he spoke to his father she would stand by him.

'We are only shallow because our customs do not allow us to go off and educate ourselves. Our education is the pianoforte and knitting. Do you men think we enjoy it? I would love to travel the world and have conversations with the King, but I am not in a position to because I am a woman.' She was now on her feet, 'and yes the customs where you came from are different. Women are not so looked down upon, but you have come home now.'

Derek's temper rose the longer Jane talked, 'You of all people should have understood Janie,' he said through clenched teeth.

'I do Derek, believe me I do. Where will she stay? You know there is no decent inn between here and...'

'Where she will stay will be my problem,' he cut her off.

'Derek, please do not be that way,' she walked over to him and took his hands but he was stiff. 'I know more than anything you have always desired to be wed to woman who could hold you to an argument, but they way you are handling this is not...'

'English?' his blue eyes, fiery, looking down at her. 'I never thought you were one to judge a man on where he came from.'

'Proper,' she corrected him. 'I am not judging her Derek...'

He held up his hand and took a step back, 'you have always locked yourself in this room and hidden behind books only talking to your family. Do not tell me you understand my plight. You do not know what it is like to find someone you want to spend the rest of your life with. You do not know what it is like to love someone you do not have to. And you most certainly do not know what it is like, to find and be in love, so do not tell me you understand me. For you are farther from my understanding than I was led to believe,' with that he left her room. The door closed with a loud bang. Jane was left standing there with Derek's words soaking into her.

# Chapter 9

E xtra lengthy, extra crispy....

William sat in his father's study, behind his father's desk. He felt the power that was emitted from the chair. He would soon be the future Duke. He would be the one making decisions. Was he ready for that commitment? Was he ready to take charge from his father? His father ran his household much like his business, with a sense of diplomacy. He and Camille were fine specimen of children. He had instilled in the good morals and values. Camille would make a fine Duchess some day or hopefully a Mariochness.

His mind wandered to Jane. She had walked away from him twice leaving him with unfinished conversations and unanswered questions. She was as timid as society thought. He wondered if she would ever let their time together grow from a mere matter of minutes. He had a feeling she was the kind of woman you could fight with, an intellectual fight where facts worked in way of points. She had fire within her that he now felt he wanted to see. He wanted to set her ablaze and be the one to calm her down. He wanted to crawl under her skin to the point she exploded. He wanted to see her at her worst. But first he had to finalize on his business.

It was a matter of urgency. He was fortunate the ton had not found out. With nosey neighbors walking all over London, they watched his every move. He had heard himself being talked about. It amazed him the time people put aside to gossip. That was the reason the economy struggled, there were more people gossiping than working. The men of society had turned into women, listening for anything that would discredit their opponents in the eyes of the shallow and baseless women.

He had kept himself private and the only one who knew what he was holding to himself, ever so close to his chest, was his dear friend Jasper. William sunk lower on the chair and closed his eyes. His age had been his downfall at the time. He should have listened to Jasper that night. He should have thought it through, but he was far too intoxicated and the pomp of Dukedom awaiting him was swimming in his head. He felt untouchable. Powerful. He didn't realize time would move on and he would grow. He would become a man who would hold responsibility. Now he had to disappear for a while so his father would never find out and he would not soil Camille's name and ruin her chances of making a match worthy of her title.

William felt guilty. He would cost his family so much if his plan did not work. His father would surely disown him and the title would go to one who did not deserve it. He was also sure Jane was a woman he wanted to know. He was enchanted by her. But he would subject her to a fate that she was not prepared for. He had to make sure he did not compromise anyone in his life first before advancing on.

There was a knock on the door, William grunted. He was not in mood to have any conversations with anyone. He much rather preferred if he could be left alone for the rest of the day. He had contemplated calling on Jane but thought better of it. It would do him no good, not when his mind was occupied with other things. The knock came again, this time a little more forceful.

William cursed under his breath and walked to the door. He opened it and took a step back. The person looking back at him was the last person he ever thought he would see again. 'Hello William, aren't you going to embrace your wife?' she asked, before pursing her blood red lips. Her dark brown eyes seeming darker than usual.

He couldn't move, couldn't speak. What was she doing here? He was the one to go to her. He had already planned his journey and Jasper would accompany him. Why had she come here? 'Come now, dear husband are you not going to let into my study?' she asked before sweeping past him and placing herself on the chair on the opposite side of the desk.

'I must say, what possessed you to get a house in Devonshire, doesn't your father own the whole of Sussex?

'What are you doing here?' William asked after he regained his composure. She changed his plans.

'I came here to continue the hoax you arranged all those years ago. We did promise each other if we were both unmarried at this time,' she let the sarcasm drip from her words and looked the least bit remorseful about it when William squared his eyes at her.

'I was supposed to come to you,' he ground out, trying his utmost best not lose his thinnning patience.

'Well I got tired of waiting. Because that is all I ever do where you are concerned William, I wait. And I got tired of waiting,' she replied calmly. An opposite of his temper which only made him angrier. 'Oh come now William, that look on your face is highly unnecessary. If you are worried I will tell your dear father and mother and that harlot you seem to have taken interest in about the child you forced me to be rid of, you needn't worry. I am your wife and my loyalty lies with you. That is of course unless you have forgotten,' she smiled at him as she took off her gloves in the most seductive way she knew how. She had won the conversation, she knew judging from the expression on his face. All she had to do was draw at his guilt.

When her informant had told her William had called on Jane after attending the ball. She was certain he was looking to explore romance with her and she would let that happen over her dead body. She was tired of being locked up, tired of being his secret. She had called herself his dear friend for far too long. She had sacrificed so much for this man all in hopes of becoming the future Duchess of Sussex. She had worked too hard to let some mute, plain girl take her place. She could have his heart and share his bed if she wanted but that title was hers.

She watched William try to come to terms with his current situation. He was a handsome man with his golden eyes that shone when he smiled and she noticed he hadn't changed his ways when it came to shaving. She had always loved men who liked to look like men. Not like that scrawny thing she had the unfortunate luck of being attached to for the rest of her days. But she would not think of that for now. Right now she had to ensure she held onto her status as his wife and use it against him to her advantage if need be.

'You will not be staying here. We are in London and people here have far more to say.'

'You want to put me up at an inn William, have you lost your mind?' she rose from the chair. 'Your parents have retired to the country, I could be your cousin,' she walked to him, running her hand over the collar of his shirt, 'like old times. Remember how much of a good time we had. I would like to relive a few of those nights.' She leaned in close and took in his scent.

William pushed her back disgusted by her lack of remorse on the matter that occurred between them. 'What do you want?'

She smiled taking a step toward him, 'what you promised me,' she whispered against his lips before planting a kiss on them. 'A title.'

**

Jane sat atop her horse, Richard looking at her as though he wanted to say something. She had been so stern with him, it shocked him. Never had his mistress ever spoken to him that way. She was usually shy and soft spoken. But not today. 'Are you sure you'll be alright?' she didn't answer, she kicked her horse and off she went.

Richard, the stable hand, could only stare after her. 'Is that Jane?' Derek asked from behind him.

'Yes, master,' Richard answered without turning around. He and Derek were like friends. Before Derek was shipped off to school, he and Richard would play for hours on end. His father had given up on ordering Richard out of Derek's room in the mornings. He had come to accept his son was a free soul and didn't see his family's title as something that would set him apart from the rest.

'She is quite the temper, master.'

'I know,' Derek said running his hand through his hair. He and Jane had had one too many fights and they always ended with him saying something he regretted. He hadn't meant to say the things he said and now with the arrival of Leila in a few hours he needed his sister there with him when their fathers temper rose. 'Get me a horse Richard,.'

This made Richard turn around. 'But master, you can barely ride.' It had been an unspoken truth between the two men that Richard was a far better rider than Derek. Derek did not hold it against him, he recognized talent when he saw it and the man before him at this time was far more skilled than he could ever hope to be.

'We all learn someday,' he said looking in the direction Jane and her horse had disappeared. He needed to apologize to her.

**

Jane pulled the reins and the horse came to a stop. She heard the gentle sound of the water in the distance. This was her favorite place, before her sister was born she and her mother would ride out in the afternoons and spend them sitting by the water, enjoying the freshness of the air. She had grown to love it and even after Sarah she still rode out on Sunday afternoons. No one knew of this place, it was her refuge.

She slid off her horse and tied it to a nearby tree. She walked steadily towards the water making sure not to slip on any of the rocks that lined the path to the stream. Once she reached, she took off her slippers and her gown followed. It was a humid day and the feel of water on her skin was just what she needed. She dipped her foot in the water, it was warm.

Once fully immersed she turned on her back and played around in the water. Moving around slowly, causing ripples to form on the surface. She was at peace here. William's face flashed through her mind. His beautiful eyes that held so much mischief when he smiled. His perfect scent, it wasn't like most men who smelled of coffee or whiskey, he smelt like fresh air. Never was there any sweat attached to him even in the heat of the day. She smiled to herself. Feeling the strength of his arms on her while they were dancing.

She wished he would appear and hold her, spin her around and let her fall in his arms. His voice was rough but manly and his accent, the French in him made him all the more attractive. 'oh Stop it Jane,' she said as she walked out of the water, her light chemise clinging to her skin. 'That man could never love you, you are simply an amusement to him because you are so silent and no one truly knows you.' She set herself down by a tree that allowed enough sunlight to spread over her but providing a good amount of shade.

'He will simply get bored when a woman far prettier than you comes by, for you are simply plain. Even these eyes papa says are so enchanting do no work for me,' she huffed. Jane was quiet but it was not by choice. She had once been a rather outspoken child, but an argument with Derek had sent her into a world of silence. He pointed out her lack of knowledge and everyone would see that every time she opened her mouth. She had sworn no one would ever hear her opinion outside of her family and it had worked in her favor. Men never bothered her at balls or stopped her on the streets of London. She was free to watch life.

But she admitted it was a lonely existence. She thought back to her conversation with Sarah, she did wonder what it felt like to be swept away by passion and love. She longed to know the feel of a touch of love.

'Your seasons are over,' she said to herself. 'You are now on the shelf.'

'Why would a beautiful woman like you say such a thing to herself?' the man standing behind her spoke. Jane jumped to her feet trying to conceal her nearly naked body. Her chemise provided little cover and it was still wet, parts of it clinging to her body. 'Please, I didn't mean to startle you. I was passing by and heard your monologue,' he smiled.

Jane scowled at him, it was not funny what he had just said. She looked about for where she had dropped her dress. 'That is not funny.'

'Forgive me.'

'Will you please turn around!'

Matthew smiled and turned around, 'I hope I have not interrupted anything.'

Jane was too busy pulling on her dress to answer his question. This was it, Her father would demand she marry this man. Why had they not insisted on her having a chaperone? Surely if she were with someone else they would have seen this intruder. She stopped. Where could he possibly be coming from? Their estate went for miles. He had to have been on their property to have found the stream.

Fear gripped her, what if he was here to kidnap her or worse, kill her? She tied the lace on the front of her dress but it wasn't holding. She cursed inside, how on earth did those women who could not afford governesses dress? She let out a breath before looking at her intruder. He had a beautiful build and his hair was black as night. 'Excuse me,' he turned around, he was smiling. He must have known what her question was because he took two sift steps towards her and turned her around, pulling the lace from her grip and began looping it through the holes. 'Thank you,' she mumbled. He pulled the lace a squeal came out of the mouth.

'It is my utmost pleasure,' he knotted the lace into a bow shaped tie. It was tight, he could see her hand over her stomach like she couldn't breathe. 'Is it tight enough?'

'Yes,' she stepped away from him. She couldn't breathe. 'Where may I ask did you learn to do that?' her hand was still on her stomach, she was trying to keep steady.

'I have a sister, she never could get anything done on her own,' his eyes smiling like he knew what she was going through, what he had done.

Jane gave up, she tried pulling at the lace but she couldn't untie it. 'Could you please,' she turned around. His hands slowly worked on untying the knot he had made. She smelled ever so sweet. 'I was wondering,' he began, 'what you are doing out here on your own without a chaperone.'

'I was wondering what you are doing out here at all,' she turned back to him relieved to have air flowing through her lungs once again.

'Forgive me, my name is Matthew, I am Lady Charlotte's brother. I have the unfortunate luck to be chaperoning my sister today. Her governess is sick.'

'Lord Matthew, that still does not explain what you are doing out here,' her eyes moved around their surroundings.

He smiled, 'no of course it doesn't. My apologies. My sister and your sister have far too much gossip to catch up on. I took a walk.'

'This is a rather far distance for a walk, Lord Matthew,' she started feeling nervous. Was this man who he really said he was? She had never heard Sarah mention Charlotte's brother. 'And my sister has never spoken of you.'

'Because my sister does not speak of me.'

'How convenient,' she looked around. They were all alone. Damn Derek and his tongue for sending her running off like this. Now she was stuck with a strange, attractive man.

'I speak the truth, you needn't be afraid of me. I know your father and I do not wish to raise his anger. I have heard stories,' he paused when Jane squinted. It was the most beautiful action he had ever seen, making her eyes look like crystal slits. 'If you wish I shall leave you alone.'

'I suggest you do it speedily,' Derek's voice sounded. He came from behind a bush. He positioned himself in front of Jane.

Jane rolled her eyes. Of course Derek had followed her so he could accost her when she was alone and convince her he did not mean his words. She preferred to be terrified from the pit of her stomach with this stranger than be in the company of her brother. His words had hurt her. His truth cut through her like a knife.

'I do not need your help Derek,' Jane scolded from behind him.

'Be quiet Jane.'

'Do not tell me to be quiet when you followed me here for the same purpose, to accost me and trap me so that I may listen to your excuse of an apology for what you said to me, is that not right?' This made Derek turn around. Jane's words had slapped him hard.

'I said those things because I was angry.'

'You said them because that is what you and mama and papa and Sarah believe. You believe me so afraid of life. Don't you think every day I wish I could be like the rest of you? Laughing and talking with people of the ton. Do you not think I wish I could swing my hair like Sarah and have men falling at my feet? I wish I could, every day.'

'Jane,' Derek said silently. He tried to hold her hand but she took a step back and turned from him. She always did this when she was about to cry. 'I spoke without thinking.'

'And that is why I do not speak Derek, because I do think.'

Derek knew he was going to get nowhere with his sister, not like this. Matthew cleared his throat, knowing they had all but forgotten him. He and his sister rarely fought, they barely spoke. She was far younger than he was and he found her constant fascination with fashion annoying. She spoke of nothing but men and clothes. His mother had tried to make them do more together, such as a visit to a friend of hers, but it was the same conversations.

The coach ride had been quiet. All she did was sigh and gasp while looking out the window. Matthew found more wisdom in a book he had carried. Once they had arrived Charlotte had run off and he found something to occupy him. He often read while moving about in his father's study. His mother said it was something his grandfather did and annoyed her to no end. He had opened his book and just walked.

Watching this brother and sister argue before him, made him feel like he had missed out on something important with Charlotte. 'Please do excuse me for interrupting but I feel, miss, your brother is rather sorry for whatever he said.'

'Of course you're going to take his side. You men will defend each other to the death.' Jane fumed. Who was this stranger who felt the need to come in between an argument that did not concern him in the least bit. She picked up her slippers and stormed off in a huff leaving both men in her wake of anger.

'She is not at all what the ton believe her to be, is she? Matthew asked.

'Nowhere near, now who may I ask who are you? Derek's tone changed.

'Lord Matthew,' he spoke bowing, 'brother to Lady Charlotte currently involved in serious gossip with your dear sister.

Derek smiled understanding exactly why Matthew had traveled out this far. He too could never stand when Sarah began her monologue of the gossip.

~口

# Chapter 10

By the time Matthew and Derek reached the house the skies were getting darker. They had stayed out by the stream, Derek missing the conversation of a young male who shared his views, opinions and feelings on certain matters and Matthew simply curious as to who Jane really was. He enjoyed spending time with his sister but some things only another man can understand. Matthew had spoken of Charlotte and all her annoying habits, but he spoke to her with a fondness in his voice. He would do anything for his sister, but she was a rather tough one to handle. All she ever thought about was men and the one's she could marry. He lacked intelligent insight from another human. His parents, he loved them dearly, were as equally as mad as his sister. His mother would pester him about finding a wife and giving her grandchildren so she could finally die in peace knowing their family line is not going to end. His father was simply concerned about a title. Matthew had to leave a son to carry on the family title.

He had accepted to escort Charlotte this day, for he needed a break from his mother's prodding. He had talked to one girl at a ball and she was already picking out names for their children. He found it insane. How could a whole society focus only on one thing, having children?

'There must be more to things to life,' he said to Derek as they walked through the doors. His question was quickly answered as Sarah and Charlotte came screeching out of a door. Men, men and more men, that was all those girls talked about. They dashed past their brothers screaming of a new arrival in London. Matthew was sure his mother was going to send him along with Charlotte hoping he would find a wife while she was making their parents proud.

'Do stay for dinner, and you may both stay for the night as well, the both of you, Derek offered to Matthew, 'it is already night time, I am sure your parents wouldn't want you riding home in the dark and besides you may just find a wife here. There is a range of women in this household,' he joked.

'As interesting as it would be, my dear mother would go mad if her Charlotte did not spend the night in her bed. She may want us married, but she is far too attached to propriety I am afraid. Perhaps you could send a formal invitation,' Jane was coming down the stairs, Matthew's words trailed off as he watched her, 'it would be rude to decline,' he said absent mindedly. She was a vision. Her riding habits were long gone and in their place a beautiful white gown, no doubt worn in honour of her purity. Her hair was braided to the side and not a tinge of rose on her ever so white face. Her eyes now a distinct deep blue, unlike what they looked like before, under the sunlight.

Derek noticing the trance his sister had put his new found friend and could only be amused by it. If Jane only knew what she inspired in men. If he wasn't her brother he would surely join the line of men who'd mentioned what a beauty his sister was. He now felt more remorseful than ever. He didn't mean the things he had said to her, and knowing dear Jane she was not ready for an apology. Another trait the ton had no idea of. It was a wonder how calm and timid they thought she was. He and their father were the only ones who knew what it felt like when one inspired wrath in Lady Jane Samantha Weldrake.

'Leaving so soon?' her voice brought him back from his thoughts. She was standing beside him but far enough to make sure their bodies made no contact whatsoever.

'I am afraid the sun does not permit the pleasure of your company any longer Lady Jane,' Matthew replied.

'Please call me Jane, Lady makes me feel far too old and you are no longer a mad man lurking in the bushes.' She smiled. She would have much to write about in her diary this night. Matthew was quite the gentleman, he had snuck up on her but kept his gentry manners. She was not one to judge based on the rules of society but if she would have, Matthew would have passed the bar.

'Now where is that dear sister of mine,' his question was answered as the screeching girls came into the parlor, still giggling amongst themselves. 'Charlotte I'm afraid you will have to save your gossip for another time.'

Charlotte stamped her foot in a huff and turned to Sarah, 'I told you he was a bore,' she turned to her brother, 'why can't you be more like Derek here. He lets his sisters do whatever they want.'

Jane looked back and forth between Sarah and Charlotte, she was thankful she had passed that age rather sane. Her sister was far too shallow and it was something that embarrassed her to no end. Though now, she found comfort in the fact that there was someone else baring her same exact shame. By the look on Matthew's face he disapproved of his sister's lack of discretion.

'You know your mother Charlotte,' he said with a tone so stern, her expression changed. She whispered a quick goodbye to Sarah and ran out the door.

'Well, Derek, it was a good talk. Lady Jane, Lady Sarah, I bid you farewell,' he bowed and followed his sister out the door.

Sarah looked between her siblings and they both looked rather upset, she was never one to solve other people's problems and besides right now she had a problem of her own. The soldiers had arrived back in London and she was positive she would find a more than suitable match in a soldier. She ran off to find her father. She was sure Derek and Jane wouldn't mind accompanying her. And Jane was so much like their mother, she would not miss a scolding.

'Jane,' Derek started. 'I know what I said to you before was rather mean, and you know I did not mean it. You are my sister and the one I come to when I have problems because you are level headed and you see what the rest of us are blind to. I know you are only thinking of what is best for your big brother.'

Jane stayed silent for a moment. She wanted to weigh her words before she spoke. 'You are engaged to be married, to a woman we have never met. I do not care where she is from Derek, all I care about is you do it the right way,' she placed her hand on her brothers.

'Sometimes I feel mama and papa lied to us, you must be the first born of this family.'

'That is highly impossible Derek, I found you here. She must have arrived by now.'

'Yes, I arranged for her to be taken into town, tomorrow I will travel to London.'

'What will you tell papa?'

'You will accompany me Janie?' he asked, ' we must find you a groom. You are far too beautiful to live on a shelf.'

She smiled. That was her brother, always looking out for her, but in this case, there was no man would want to marry a girl who had gone through five seasons with not one proposal.

# Chapter 11

A sneak into the past of Lady Constance Seymour, i'll let you all decide whether to be #teamwilliam or #teammatthew

Enjoy...xoxo...

'Lady Constance Seymour,' he announced, she walked past him with a smile on her lips. She slithered down the stairs like the snake she was. The season in London was coming to an end. There would be one more grand ball in honour of the soldiers in a fortnight, but before then London needed to know her name. She wore red knowing full well what it meant. Her lips were painted the colour of roses and she offered quite the view of her bossom. One thing she thanked God for was her mother, her beautiful mother who had blessed her with beauty beyond what any man could imagine. Eyes had already began following her around the room as she made her way to a table at the back. The occupant was busy in a conversation with another gentleman. They each had glasses of brandy and toasted to something she didn't know. She briefly stopped when a rather dashing young man stepped in her path and offered her his hand. She placed her delicate ungloved fingers in his as he placed a kiss on the back of her hand. This was too easy with other men. She just needed one to follow suit.

He whispered something rather untoward in her ear, as exciting as it sounded, she had business to attend to. So she simply smiled and kept moving. 'Good evening William, Jasper.' They both looked shocked beyond belief.

'What are you doing here Constance?' William shot out of his chair.

'Stop all the dramatics William, unless of course you want to cause a scene. For that I am eternally prepared,' she looked around the room, 'where is that harlot of a woman you are so taken with? I suppose she and I could become great friends.'

'What do you want Constance?'

'We had this conversation William, you know exactly what I want and until I get it I will make your life a living hell. I gave up my life for you, don't you forget that,' she placed a kiss on his cheek, 'now if could please point me in the direction of a gentleman that will help me forget what a terrible man you are.'

The look of confusion on Jasper's face and the reaction William had was enough to raise a few eyebrows. Many of the older women simply assumed she was his femme fatal and was now tired of being kept in the dark. For the men she was a romance that occurred far too long ago and she wished to rekindle the flame. Many men in the room knew the problem a love scorned could do.

Lady Constance looked delectable and she enjoyed her evening. She danced with nearly every gentleman in the room, married or not. It was not her concern if a man did not admire his wife enough to stay by her side for a whole night. Marriage, as William had proven to her, was simply an idea. It didn't really exist. There was no such thing as fidelity. She believed there was a man and a woman and these two came together when they had similar interests. In her case her interest was money.

**

She had grown up poor, they barely had two coins to rub together. Despite this her mother was always smiling. She wondered where one found joy in struggling and hunger. Her father did everything he could for her and her sister, Arabella. She was Constance's everything. She taught her everything she knew. At the tender age of one and six Arabella decided she was tired of living a life of poverty and watching life pass her by. She took matters into her own hands. She turned to men, they gave her gifts and money. Constance never knew why they gave her these things. She remembered falling asleep to the sound carriages leaving her sister at their door. She always laughed and then silence.

Arabella bought food fit for kings and queens. Their mother always complained and their father simply kept his silence. For Constance, Arabella was a queen, beautiful intelligent and rich. One evening after returning home from her escapades she sat them all down and said she had found them a house and they would never starve again and she would no longer be in the company of men.

She was now one and eight. Their house was beautiful. Far more than what they had, but Arabella fell sick. She grew thinner as the days went by and her beauty began fading, Constance was at a loss. The doctors did not know what was wrong with her. They had the best physicians in all of the London look at her. Her voice became weaker and she barely ate. The night before Christmas Arabella left the world, she left her family, she left Constance behind. Her mother didn't have the heart to clear away her belongings so the task fell on her. She placed all her beautiful gowns in chests and locked them away never to be seen again.

One night before the New Year, a man finely dressed arrived in a carriage bearing the symbol of the earl called upon them, he said Arabella was his mistress and he had been away on business only to hear of her passing. He did all he could to be there before they lowered her body. He said he was in the process of leaving his wife. He gave Constance a diary that contained writings of what Arabella had always said she should have should she ever leave the world.

Constance read every page, and left tear stains on each and every one of them. Arabella knew she was ailing. The life she had lead was not a righteous one and it was far from what their mother had taught them, but she did what she had to for the family. She apologized to Constance for not being a better sister and to her mother who had wanted so much more in life for her. The house they lived in was now theirs, Arabella asked only that of the man she bedded, he accepted without hesitation. They now had the life Arabella had wanted for them, but she wasn't here to share it with them.

Constance sought refuge in her sorrow , her father turned to the bottle and gambling and everything they had was now slowly draining away and her mother sought silence for the rest of her days. Constance went back to Arabella's diary and read how she seduced the men, she unlocked the chest with her sisters clothes and decided she would become Arabella. She lived in her sister's shoes and how glorious they were. By one and seven she was the most sought after woman, until she met William. He ordered all other men to stay away from her and she became his prize possession, he gave her whatever she wanted, her father was too far gone to help, she left him in sorrow and turned away from her past. To the world she was orphaned at three and had nowhere to call home.

William gave her his heart and that was her shelter. They married in an old barn with a priest and a friend of his as a witness as the law required. He would leave her in the country and go off to London for months at a time but when he came back he always came back with gifts, far more than she could ever imagine. She fell pregnant and William had convinced her it was not time for children in their lives and she had to take care of it.

It broke her heart but she loved him and she believed he loved her too. He left for London, he left her to suffer from the pain on her own. He left her with a promise it was almost time to make her his queen, he left and he never came back. She waited for him for months. Those months turned to years, until she got tired of waiting. She opened the pages of her sister's diary and read through it again. Arabella was not one to be kept waiting and neither was she. Arabella had gone to London and attended every ball the earl had thrown. She entered his circle until he could no longer ignore her. She had written letters with instructions to be delivered if she was not to arrive at the house they lived in. Letters to his wife, to his children, to friends. The only thing 'the titles' as she called them were concerned about was keeping their names unscathed.

She promised the earl she would burn London around him if he did not give her what she wanted. Her threats finally got his attention. Constance packed her bags and went to London. She was living her sister's life, she would live it to the end.

**

The night ended and she bid her dear husband a goodnight. He had put her up in an agreeable house with a few servants. He would see her again, but first she wanted to seek out this beautiful mute woman everyone seemed to be talking about.

3N!fw$*w

# Chapter 12

------------------------------------------------------------

A new chapter guys, we're getting to know our characters a little bit better...

I'm dedicating this chapter to @Atrapadaenletras who's going to translate this book to Spanish....

Happy reading...

Jane had not slept that night. There was this unsettling feeling in her stomach. She tossed and turned till the first rays of sunlight came through her window. She had never been a light sleeper or lacked sleep at all. It was strange and when Sarah walked into her room looking well rested she felt the fatigue of a sleepless night fall over her. Sarah jumped on her bed and pulled the bedding off of her, 'Good Lord Jane how can you still be asleep, do you not see the sun outside?'

Her vision could not focus, her mind was foggy, she heard her sister speak but she was not sure what she had said. 'Janie,' Sarah shook her, 'Lord William is here to see you,' she said in her most convincing French accent. 'You must get up and try to make yourself presentable, heaven knows why you do let Rosa do anything for you, that is why mama has her. She is your governess.'

'I am a grown woman Sarah, I am not disabled or handicapped I can do things by myself.'

'Yes but papa is paying her quite the sum, he often complains she never does any work.'

'I told papa I didn't need her but he insisted. If he feels he is paying her for nothing it is of his own doing, Sarah please get off my bed. What time is it?' Jane was beginning to get irritated. She had no sleep the night before and Sarah was being exceptionally annoying this particular morning. 'Where is Derek?'

'He went to London. Lord knows I am thankful mama did not make him drag me with him. As much I would love to see the soldiers I am much more content here. There seems to be more happening in Devonshire than there is in London.'

Jane smiled to herself, if she only knew the storm coming. Derek was bringing his love home. Their father was a rather calm man but he valued what his family left to him and he in turn will leave it his son, a son who knows and respects propriety. She had no time to think of that now, Sarah had now begun bouncing on her bed.

'Sarah, for all that is holy will you please get off my bed.'

'Why are you always so uptight?' she stopped bouncing and sat on the side of her bed. 'I envy you, you know. You are intelligent. I suppose that is why William is running after you. I get only fools. If a soldier looked my way that would be very...' she didn't finish the sentence instead looked towards the window. She had their mother's features. Her face was angular, like the pretty women who sang in the bars. She always thought it was a shame they had all that beauty and yet their bodies were abused by married men who enjoyed deceiving their wives.

'Well anyway,' Sarah burst through her thoughts with her chipper spirit back, mama says you must look presentable so I am here to help you with your hair. A gentleman is used to be kept waiting. I am hoping William is a gentleman. And Charlotte and her brother have been invited for the hunting games. They shall be residing here with papa's friends.'

Jane looked at her sister, only Sarah had so much gossip before the sun had the chance to fit properly into the sky.

'He is a soldier, papa and his father are old friends,' she continued, 'well they were friends, he died. He and his mother will be residing with us. Charlotte is excited. It is better than London,' she continued her monologue as she helped Jane into her dress and added some colour to face after many a protest. Her hair was left untouched by Sarah's hands. Jane braided it and pulled it the side, leaving one strand hanging free.

William had stared at the potted plant to he point he believed he was now a part of the flowers blossoming from it. He admired the amount of time Jane took to receive him. She was not one to put too much into her attire so he assumed she was pacing about in her nervous state. He smiled to himself. He still had that effect on women. He was no longer a young man with youth being his best feature, but he was far ahead of all the other young gentlemen in society. None of them had had the thought to take interest in Jane and yet she was the most surprising woman of the ton. He was hoping for an invitation to the hunting games her father organized every year. It would provide him with the time he needed to woo her.

He would have to take care of Constance before then. He saw her fast becoming a problem in his life. A problem he could do without. Jasper had reproached him for having a wife at all. He was comfortable in the fact the priest they had used was not in fact a real priest but a young man William had found in need of a coin or two. He was bound to Constance in no way. The only misfortune she brought him was the child he had ordered out of her womb. His father would never forgive him for such a gruesome thing. Just then Jane appeared at the top of the staircase, her sister by her side. His thoughts would have to wait, at this moment he had a heart to conquer.

The breeze of the morning was rather cold, Jane wondered why anyone would choose to walk in such weather. She pulled her shawl closer to her.

'Do you enjoy this weather Lady Jane?' William asked. He had noticed her trying to cover every inch of open skin she had.

'You came all this way to ask me what kind of weather I find agreeable at this early hour Lord William?'

He smiled, there was the woman he curious to know, 'I suppose not.' They spent the rest of the morning walking through her father's gardens. They touched on many subjects, each fascinating William even more. She was far more educated than he had previously thought and certainly well read. She quoted from her heart, a talent only someone who read one thing over and over again could manage.

When she laughed it was like music to his ears, her laughter reached her eyes and they shone even brighter. The morning cold was slowly disappearing and the weather became far more agreeable for Jane. She dropped her shawl a little so it was hanging loosely on her shoulders. Her demeanor had changed, she was more open and free spirited. The ton knew nothing about Jane. She was a hidden gem.

'Why hadn't I met you sooner.' He said absentmindedly as she was picking a few flowers.

'Pardon me?' she was standing straight up her eyes locked onto his.

William could not breathe. He closed the distance between them and softly placed his lips over hers. Jane froze. She couldn't move. Sarah would be so pleased with her. When William made no attempt to step back she quickly broke their connection and placed a respectable distance between them. Her chest was rising and falling at a rate William found enchanting. He wanted to be that close to her again.

'I believe you have overstayed your welcome my Lord,' she tried to sound calm but her voice broke at every word.

'I believe I have. I look forward to an invitation from you Lady Jane.' Her confused expression made his heart stop. Why hadn't he met Jane first? If she was the one he had met in London all those years ago, he would have been married with children. 'the hunting season is almost upon us. Your father is famous for his hunting parties. I have never seen a man shoot a rifle like the great Duke of Devonshire.'

'My father never misses, that is common knowledge. I shall mention it to him Lord William. If you would please,' she gestured towards the house. He took his cue, but not before placing a kiss on the inside of her palm, the same way he had when they first met.

His hazel eyes starting a fire deep within her. The sun was now fully in place and the heat Jane was feeling, she blamed on the unpredictable weather of England. Her mother would be happy, if things went on like this, she would be married before the end of the year. William was unlike other men and the storied many told of him were so far from the truth. He did not prey on young and naïve women. His conversation was, in totality, very respectable. He never queried on matters that were none of his concern and he kept his distance, most of the time. She felt herself blushing. Thank heavens Sarah had insisted she wear a little rose on her cheeks, it would not be so obvious.

She would never be able to hide this from her sister. Sarah had a sixth sense about men. She could tell when a man has interest in a woman and she could also tell when a woman has been compromised. But in Jane's case it was hardly a compromise, she was still as pure as the day she was born, well almost as pure as the day she was born. She smelt the flowers in her hand. They would look beautiful in the parlor.

Matthew had found comfort in a bench in the gardens when he learned Derek was in London and there was no hope in him returning before sundown. Charlotte had run of screeching as always with her dear friend, over men no doubt. His mind was deep in a medical journal he did not hear Jane approaching. 'I suppose we could try another introduction with me fully clothed,' she spoke from behind him.

'Lady Jane,' he stood up quickly and as a result his book went flying across the flower bed and into the fountain.

'Oh goodness,' Jane lifted her skirts and ran to the rescue of his book, unfortunately it was soaked through by the time she managed to get it out of the water.

'I don't suppose there is dry land anywhere we could introduce ourselves politely,' the entire sleeve of her dress was drenched.

'Well,' she said as she handed him back his book, 'nowhere near I am afraid. This will have to do for now. Please sit.'

I am afraid I am at the mercy of a book for the day,' he spoke when she offered no conversation.

'Not quite Lord Matthew, my mother informed me you accompanied Charlotte, I can imagine what it is like living with her.'

'Is Sarah not the same?' he asked a little puzzled. In his opinion she made as much, if not mot more, noise than his dear sister.

'You and I are not, I have patience to deal with Sarah. I believe you are like my brother. The only time they spend in each other's company is during meals and carriage rides, in which he chooses to take a nap.'

Matthew laughed. She was humorous. 'Forgive my intrusion, but may I ask how come you are such a blossom and yet when out in society you are,' he paused looking for a word, 'silent.'

'It a choice I made.'

'Come now, no one chooses to seclude themselves to that extent. You can consider me a friend Jane. Your confidences in me will not be betrayed. At least not by me.'

She looked at him. For a moment she could not find her words, and her heart had a little flutter. 'I don't suppose you hear of a man by the name Michael Burman?' when he shook his head she was thankful. 'When I came out in my first season I was much like my sister. Eager and completely naïve. I thought every man who came to ask for a dance would be a husband by the end of the season like it happened with my cousin. I was overjoyed when he filled my dance card and I was exclusively his for the night. The whole room was sure I was to be married soon. I was a rather stupid girl back then.'

'You were inexperienced I would hardly call that stupid.'

She smiled at him and wondered why she had chosen to tell him of all people this story. They never spoke of it after it happened, her father had made sure of that. 'Yes well inexperience and stupidity are one in the same. I was so taken I did not stop to think his ever growing insistence on us spending ample time alone. My mother was not like she is today. I always had a chaperone, Rosa. She was mine and Derek's governess when we were children. I am afraid I put her out of work,' she said guiltily. Now she saw Sarah's point, 'in any case he convinced me to escape her and sneak off with him one night,' she could not seem to continue. The humiliation she had suffered at his hand was too much to bear.

She had almost lost what was most precious to her. 'You needn't go on if it is too difficult for you. It is almost time for lunch, judging from the smell of that food.'

'Don't you want to know the end of the story.'

'It is not important. Any man who would take advantage of a woman the way this Michael did, is a coward. Not worthy of mention in my books.'

Jane was left speechless. It was rare to find a man not interested in hearing the end of her story. That was all they ever asked her. She was thankful for her father's influence in society or she would still be answering questions to this day. 'And besides,' he added, 'I would rather speak of something that would make you smile. You have a beautiful smile, so I have been told.'

'And who told you that?'

'You are the most talked about belle at the ball, Lady Jane. Did you not know? Everyone waits in anticipation for your arrival and yet you never truly arrive.'

'Well, I am not a fan of dances.'

'And yet you do it so well. I saw you dance with your brother.'

'I never said I did not know how to dance, I said I am not a fan of dances.'

'In that case I am in luck. The hunting games ball is soon, once the season in London is over, your father knows how to gather all the snobbish men and women well. Save me a dance Lady Jane,' he was now standing and offering her his hand.

Jane was taken aback, just a few moments ago she was in the company of William who was by all notes a gentleman in his mannerisms except when he decided to take his liberties with her. She was glad he did, it made her feel like a real woman. The way Sarah described the lives of the saloon girls as she called them. But now here in the company of Matthew she felt every bit a lady. The same way her mother described being the company of her father when they first met. He was every bit polite and did not feel the need to converse on things that made her uncomfortable.

Jane had to tread lightly, but there was something about this man she was with now that made her want to explore what she was feeling a little bit further.

# Chapter 13



Sorry for the length, promise the next one will be longer...

Happy reading...

Charlotte and Sarah had chosen to sleep in Lord Weldrake's study as it was the largest room and offered the most privacy. They would no doubt gossip all night. Derek was yet to return from London and Jane found herself becoming more anxious as the hours passed. How would her brother explain to her father he is already engaged, to a woman they have never met. He should have mentioned it when he returned from his studies.

She had spent the rest of the day in Matthew's company, talking and laughing at the caricature their society was. He was an intelligent man and one not eager to marry and appease his father. He wanted to marry for love and love only. He did not want a wife who was raised to be a wife, he wanted a wife who was raised to be a woman. A woman with a mind of her own and an opinion that would send the men in the courts running. He did not want a wife who's vocabulary only consisted of yes, my Lord and no, my Lord. His mother was far too sharp tongued and his father had survived and been faithful to her and only her. He did not see a reason such a marriage would fail with him.

He had always wanted to be a doctor but he had to sacrifice that one thing for his family and his title. He could not be traversing the continent and dealing with his daily duties. His father had far too many businesses and he was next in line. He still read medical journals and cared for the sickly servants in his home. No one understood why but to him it was his way of practicing and fulfilling his father's wishes all at once.

Jane was impressed by him. He had a dream beyond a title and he certainly rivaled William in handsomeness. He had a smile that would send any woman's skirts flying high and a very likable personality. She considered her day well spent and she had found a friend in Matthew.

As they made their way to the balcony for a glass of wine and brandy for the men Jane felt William's soft kiss once more. She wondered when he would return. In her heart she knew she was losing her senses. How could she fall in love with a man that took his liberties with her the way William did. But how could she not. She was not one for adventure but she did not mind small doses of silent rebellion.

'Reminiscing a love I presume?' Matthew said falling into step with her.

Her blush deepened under the cover of Sarah's magic. 'Hardly, I do not know enough men to fall in love, Lord Matthew.'

'I take great offence in your words Lady Jane. We have spent the part of the day in each other's company. I am afraid I may have spent too much time in the company of women, pray tell do I sound like one?'

Jane laughed at this statement. 'I apologize. I did not mean to offend you. You do not sound like a woman, you are every bit a man. One of the most manly men I ever laid eyes on. '

'Lady Jane, seducing a man is shunned upon in our society.'

'So is comparing yourself to a woman, Lord Matthew. We are both at fault here. Whatever shall we do?' their conversation came to an abrupt end as they reached the doors of the balcony and now joined Lord and Lady Weldrake. As the norm Matthew went off to her father to talk about business over a glass of brandy and she and her mother sat admiring the skies.

It was a beautiful night. She wished she could walk about the gardens under the watchful eyes of the stars.

'Look at that dear, your last season and men are falling at your feet. Lord William was here rather early. I saw the both of you disappear into the gardens. I hope he respected you.' Lady Weldrake noticed the blush on her daughters cheeks and knew the warning would come to late. 'I do not send you about with a chaperone because I believe you to be an intelligent young lady. Do not be swayed by sweet actions Jane. Remember a man is still a man, and he should be able to spend time with you in the presence of your family, not secluding you away.'

'Yes, mama. I know. He only kissed me.' Lady Weldrake stiffened. 'Mama, I am far wiser than I was all those years ago.'

'That man has a reputation Janie, please be careful. Rosa will now be accompanying you and I do not want to hear your protests or I will have your father give the order.'

Jane stopped whatever complaint she had prepared. If her father was to become aware of what transpired he would lock her away forever. Matthew and her father seemed to be having quite the time in each other's company. They had refilled their glasses twice. And now in a much merrier mood. The business talk faded away and now they were being men criticizing the society and the balls and the women. Jane was blessed to have her family. She needed to tread carefully with William. She felt herself slipping back to her old ways. It would not do at all.

3

# Chapter 14

---

William rode back to London with great haste. He did not want Constance causing a stir in the society. Her appearance had already raised enough eyebrows and one too many people had noticed their altercation at the ball, gossip spread fast in England, but it always seemed to spread faster in London. He had asked Jasper to take command over her, but he knew his wife, she was never one to listen to reason. He hoped Jasper was able to entertain her enough for her not to want to gallivant around town. He stopped in front of his town house and looked about for any wandering eyes. He envied his friend, his discretions were not followed as William's. He had the liberty to break a heart and it would not taint him in any way.

Being confident no wandering eye had wandered in his direction he burst through the doors to be met with a flying pot and fleeing man servant. He took a deep breath. It was going to be difficult to cut all ties with Constance. He was not legally bound to her but she knew enough about him to bring ruin to him and his family.

'William,' Constance screeched when she laid eyes on him, 'this is unacceptable, you cannot lock me away in this house. I cannot leave. The servants won't let me leave.' She composed herself, 'I did not leave where I was a prisoner to become a prisoner in another place, surely will you have mercy on me,' she said to no one in particular.

'You should not have left where you were in the first place Constance, I told you I would come to you and I have never broken my word.'

'Yes, but you started courting another woman and that will just not do.'

'Would you believe me if I told you I was in love with her?' he asked hoping he would anger enough, but the words surprised him. How could he fathom such a feeling, love was for the weak minded. Jane was the daughter of a Duke and he was the son of a Duke and a French woman as far as he was concerned. He needed a pure Duchess, one mild enough for society and fiery enough for the private quarters. Jane seemed like the kind of woman who would not be timid after vows were said. If beauty were added to the equation, she had an appearance that was manageable. He had stolen a kiss from her and hoped it would give her sleepless nights. Enough of them for him to propose and leave her no room to turn down his hand. But before any of that could happen he needed to ensure Constance was no longer a bother.

'You would not recognize love if it slapped you in the face William, please do not speak so foolishly. It does not beget your current title. And I do not want to be the Duchess attached to the fool of a Duke. Now where is Jasper, I believe now that you have graced us with your presence I may leave this dreary house for a few hours.'

'Everything you want is in this house Constance, what need have you joining the rest of society?'

'A lady, William, always has needs. Mine are not meant in this hell, I must seek them elsewhere, shall I tell your servants to fetch me a carriage?' it was not a question merely an indication that she would leave whether he wanted her to or not.

After the soldiers welcome ball, he would take her back Sussex and lock her away. He would declare her insane and she would never see the light of day. He would then be free to marry Jane and secure himself a beautiful business partnership and save his family's name from shame. He would not ruin his sister's marriage cart.

**

It was the second time Maria had seen Derek walking about town with a woman. She was strange, she did not seem like she was familiar with the city and the people. She smiled at everything and her features were rather plain. She did not look like she was from an aristocrat family. The way he walked with her, was like they were engaged. He held her hand and all the time not minding the stares that followed them as they passed. Maria was angered. She had her eyes on the future Duke of Devonshire, who was this woman trying to take her place? It was not only because her mother had insisted she marry a Duke, she found Derek quite handsome, with his blue eyes and beautiful appearance. He did not look like the other men. They all had the same face, they would hide who they really were until they married you. Then they would leave you to take care of their children while they go about gambling and bedding other women. That is what their father did and because of him, she is here selling her body to any man willing to pay the highest price.

Women like her rarely had a happy ending. They gave men what they wanted hoping one would make an honest woman out of them but the men were only after their bodies. Maria watched them stop by a florist. The lady smiled ever so brightly when Derek handed her a red rose. She put it to her nose and said something which in turn made him smile.

When would she find a soul willing to do for her what the men she had bedded did for other women? Age was not on her side and her beauty would soon fade. She was a year away from being too old to be on the marriage mart and not one man had looked her way. Her heart sank as she watched them steal a kiss behind a bouquet Derek was now holding.

Her mother had caused her ruin, she had insisted she befriend as many a man as her beauty would allow her. She knew they talked about her at the gentleman's club. Exchanging notes on how well to please her.

'Maria, stop staring at nothing and start looking for a man that will save us from ruin,' her mother scolded from behind her.

'What is the point of it all mother, you do not love me anymore than you loved father. There are no men in this town who would marry a woman who has walked around all of London, no' she smiled, 'England, all of England. All so that her mother can continue to attend balls and be respected. My body is worthless and the men do not care what is in my head. So why mother? Why am I looking for a man?' She now turned to her mother whose face always wore the same look, indifference. 'I can bring you money if that is what you want, but do not hold a candle for my wedding day.'

'Oh please, Maria, now is not the time for dramatics. The Duke of Sussex wants nothing to do with you. His father made that quite clear. His fool of a friend does not want your hand either. He is a Marquis' son. A mere Marquis. And it looks like the Duke of Devonshire is spoken for. The soldiers will be here in a few days time. Possibly you could tickle the fancy of one of them. Maria,' she scolded when she realized her daughter's attention had been stolen, 'get your head out of the clouds. There is nothing like love. There is only gain and advantage where every marriage is concerned.'

Maria had long stopped listening to her mother. She knew there were marriages that were full of love and respect and that is what she wanted for herself. She would see to it that she got it. She watched Derek enter a shop with his beloved laughing and smiling, she too would have that whatever it took.

**

'When do I get to meet your family Derek?' my mama told me all about England. Your father is a Duke you say. I read all I could on the Duke's I do believe I know enough to hold a conversation with one.'

Derek laughed. She was a beauty but far too innocent for this society. He feared she would not settle as fast as he had hoped. The customs across the sea were far different from theirs. They did not have Kings and Queens or Dukes and Duchesses. It was not common for an unmarried woman to be seen in the presence of the Duke, alone. He would have Jane school her on the decorum of English society.

He now saw her worry and concern. Many would see her as disrespectful and his father as mild tempered as he was, was still a Duke and he would do nothing to taint a name he was far too proud of. He would take her back to Devonshire, in hopes he and Jane would be able to resolve this situation.

'It does not quite work that way Leila. Unmarried women do not speak to the Duke's openly, married women do no such thing either.'

'Isn't he family?'

'Yes, but not quite yet. There are certain standards to be met before one can become acquainted with the Duke on a personal level.'

'You speak of your father as if he is a King. Do you speak to him?

'Of course he is my father.'

'And he will soon be my father, so I do not see a problem,' she turned her attention to something, in her opinion, more jovial, I want to go to a ball, and dance with a prince.'

think of Derek later, now she needed to get Sarah off of her bed. 'Come on Janie, won't you say you will. Please. The soldiers are arriving today and tomorrow Charlotte and I would like to go into town. She says they will not be staying in London. And there are quite a few who reside in Devonshire, please Janie say you will come with us. Papa will never allow us to go on our own and you do not require a chaperone.'

Her sister was wrong. Rosa would be accompanying her everywhere she went from now on. Since William had stolen a kiss from her, her mother had insisted. He had not called upon her again, but it not stop the fluttering in her stomach every time someone mentioned his name.

'And Matthew,' she continued, 'will be escorting his sister.

'Very well dear sister. I shall accompany you, but not tomorrow, papa is receiving a guest and we must be here to give him a warm welcome.'

'But we do not even know him.'

'Sarah, one day when you are older, you will understand why manners are required in a household.'

'Manners, manners,' she said rising from the bed.

'You will be married one day and you will remember this conversation.'

'Yes mother, she rolled her eyes and left the room.

Jane was nervous. She had not seen Matthew for a few days and she was eager to be in his company. He was very easy to talk to and his smile was the most genuine smile she had ever seen. He would make a woman very happy when he finally decided to take a wife. They had talked of marriage, but he was not optimistic he would find a woman he could live with for the rest of his days. All the ones he had had the unfortunate pleasure of meeting were either title seekers or far too stupid for his taste. She had agreed with him on that point. She would watch the women at balls, they would swarm to the men like bees to a flower.

'Janie,' Sarah burst through the door once again. 'He's here.'

'Good Lord Sarah, who is here?'

'William. Duke of Sussex. He is here to see you. You will soon be married is I assure you.' Then her face fell. Jane was now straightening her bed covers.

'What is the matter?'

'Nothing,' Sarah jumped. Please do hurry. Mama says it not good decorum to keep a man waiting too long. He may lose interest. In my opinion if a man truly wants you he will wait as long as it takes. And Janie,' she said before leaving, 'wear your lavender dress. Your eyes will look simply pleasant.'

Jane descended the staircase, William was waiting by the front door. He looked rather handsome, draped in black from head to toe. She had never seen a man look as handsome as this one in front of her did. When he heard her he turned around and she almost missed a step. A smile ever so pleasant spread across his face. He walked to the staircase and he reached out for her. His hand was warm and welcoming.

The contact with his skin sent tingles all along her body. She hoped they would be able to steal a few moments alone and he would repeat his indecent act. She quite liked it. Rosa appeared suddenly and all hope of that left her.

'Good Morning, Lord William.'

'Please, call me William, Lord is not a title I can claim as mine yet, Lady Jane.' There was a glint in his eyes. She could not tell what it was but she was happy she saw it. She turned to Rosa who was waiting patiently. She had no authority to send her off. They would simply have to walk a little faster than usual or send Rosa looking for a rose. She smiled to herself.

'Shall we please, the weather is quite pleasant today, I was hoping we would go into town and walk about for an hour or so. I shall have you back before night fall.'

'Yes, William,' she let him lead her to the carriage. She sat beside Rosa and directly opposite to William.

He kept his eyes on her the whole journey, making small conversation, not wanting to reveal his thoughts in front of their escort. When they finally reached town, it had felt like a day's journey. He helped her out the carriage and Rosa kept a safe distance but close enough not to lose sight of her mistress. They walked about the town looking at nothing in particular. Entering store after store and laughing at each other's sarcastic comments.

William had traced a path for them to follow and soon enough they would lose their escort and he would do what he had been waiting to do since he laid eyes on Jane this morning. He was becoming far too fond of her. He felt his heart losing the battle to his mind. He needed her to fall in love with him, not the other way around. He found himself enjoying the shine of her eyes when she laughed and the upper crease of her mouth when she laughed. She would gaze at something she liked ever so intently and not notice he was watching her.

For the things she found repulsive, because she was every bit a lady, she would simply squint her eyes a little and move on. There was a look in her eyes, however, he had not yet mastered. She would look about the people and almost recognize someone then it was gone. Who was she looking for? He knew she was far to timid to leave her home, the only way she would be in someone's company was if someone called upon her. He would have to find out who has been occupying her time.

They moved on to the last store. William led her through the different isles and soon enough, he looked back and there was no Rosa. He had finally lost her. He led to the back door, with little protest from her. 'I finally have to myself,' he whispered in her ear before crashing his lips to hers.

It was the sweetest feeling she had ever felt. He smelt like a man, it was not an offensive odor, unlike most men, who smelled like they had not seen a bath in weeks. His face was smooth and clean. There was no hair anywhere to cause an irritation for her. She enjoyed the moment far too much. Her hands found their way to his neck, her fingers circling the small hairs on the back of his head.

William could tell she was enjoying this as much as he was. The motion her fingers were making was driving him insane. He wanted more of her, but not yet. He reluctantly pulled away from her. She followed him after their lips had parted. They were both breathing hard and unsteady. Jane's lips were slightly swollen from the kiss. She opened her eyes and William felt his breath leave him. He could not construct a sentence in his mind, he could not move his lips. Her eyes.

They held so much passion, he felt himself drowning in them. The ever sweet blue had turned to a stormy sea and the black center was ever so small it almost looked like she had none. He could not imagine what they would look like after, the door opened.

'Lady Jane,' Rosa spoke startled at the small distance between the two bodies. She noticed her mistress's demeanor. 'I believe it about time we leave.' She knew she had spoken out of turn but she knew of her mistress's history and was not going to let it happen again. She preferred when she kept the company of the young gentleman that called upon them with his sister. He always had their conversations in the presence of others and was never too generous with his hands. The Duke and Duchess liked him a great deal as well, unlike this man who would remove her mistress from the company of others. He had not spoken to her parents about his intentions and yet here he was taking his liberties with her.

'I apologize, your lady is right Lady Jane, it is about we leave. I promised to deliver you back before night fall,' he stepped past Rosa, leaving the two ladies in each other's company.

'My Lady I know I am but your maid, but may I please speak freely,' she did not wait for Jane's reply, 'there is something untoward about that man. I pray, be careful.'

Jane had no reply, her mind was still full of his kiss. She would still feel his lips on hers. Hers were burning for more. She wanted him to ask for her hand so she would be at liberty to kiss him as much as she wanted without having to worry about what the rest of society thought. And she would not need an escort to be with her when she was walking with her husband.

The word in itself made her smile. She was ready for marriage. Her last season and this is what it held. If she would have known she would have stopped attending balls a long time ago. Jane looked at Rosa and followed the path William had taken. Rosa had spoken out of turn. She did not know what it felt like to be in love. Jane was sure she was in love. She thought of William when she rose and his face was her lullaby. The mention of his name felt like small sparks lighting in her body.

Rosa followed behind them, hoping Jane would take heed to her words for she was not the only one watching the couple.

The carriage came to a stop and William stepped to meet Lady Weldrake waiting for them. The look on her face was stern, unlike the usual jovial look she wore.

Jane stepped out after him and froze. Her mother was upset, but she had done nothing wrong. She had taken Rosa with her. They had been in her sights for the length of their excursion, for most of it.

Lord William,' she said unsmilingly. He bowed and waited for her to speak. 'I am afraid it is far too late an hour to be bringing back an honorable woman.

'I do apologize Lady Weldrake, 'time seemed to escape us and the pleasure of your daughters company is the biggest distraction. I do apologize.

The Duchess eyed him, she was not sure whether he was speaking truth. She looked at her daughter as she stepped out the carriage assisted by a footman, Jane looked rather flushed and Rosa who followed behind her had a glare set on William's back. She knew something had transpired between her daughter and the man before her. He had again taken his liberties with her and Jane was none the wiser. Had she not learned her lesson? She was far too quick to trust, that was her only flaw. She was a good judge of character but failed to see when one was not being truthful with her.

'I thank you for returning her, Rosa, you may retire. Lord Cartwright, I believe you have overstayed your welcome.'

'Of course,' he bowed once more before retreating back into the carriage. Lady Weldrake waited until it was a safe distance away before she turned on her daughter. Jane was far too shy to look up at her mother. She knew just one look she had been discovered.

'Mama, it is not that late. The sun has not left the sky.'

'No it hasn't Jane, but you certainly left your senses elsewhere. Why did Rosa look to your guest with such hatred?' before Jane could form an answer a carriage came into view. The horses affront were coming with such speed and determination.

It stopped and the door swung open, a brown eyed girl jumped from the carriage and ran for the Duchesses prized roses, she bent over an emptied the contents of her stomach. The Duchess looked back and forth from the just emerged Derek and Jane.

'What is the meaning of this Derek? Who is that girl?'

'My fiancée mother,' Derek said as he looked to Leila was now standing with her hand firmly on her stomach and her face looking quite stricken

=

# Chapter 16

----------------------------------------

Dedicated to

Check out her amazing work, Chester's Photography

Here's a new chapter...enjoy

xoxox....

Jane was standing in the center of her father's study like she was in the courts for treason. Her mother was standing behind her father, who was seated on his chair. The look in his eyes was more of anger than disappointment and for that she was thankful. Derek had escaped this trial for his newly discovered fiancée had to settle in, she was given a room next to Jane's.

'This William,' her father spoke. He never addressed men he had no respect for with titles. She knew William would have to move the heavens if her father was to accept him as her husband. A question she was yet to hear him ask. The kiss they had shared, to Jane was more than enough to convince her she was to be betrothed very soon. 'He too took you to town and took his liberties with you.'

'No father he did not,' she would not let William be blamed for an action she was more than willing to commit to as well. 'We were both...'

'Silence, Jane. You know this has happened before and yet you to do not take heed of the signs of a story passed repeating itself. You are too grown to be  believing love is love and people are not dishonest. You are the best judge of character in this house. You kept your brother from marrying a woman who was only seeking fortune. But when it comes to discerning who is right and wrong for you, it seems to me you are blind.' To this she had no response, because she knew it was true.

'Your mother tells me she insisted Rosa go with you whenever you leave, but she is not required to do that anymore because you will not be leaving the gates anytime soon. I expected to be doing this to Sarah, not you, but you have left me no choice. If this William wants to see you he must do it in our presence. There is nothing honorable about a man who hides a woman so he can take his liberties with her. It was only the other day he refused the hand of a very beautiful prospect. A woman, it was brought to my attention, he had been showing affections to.'

'But papa, I love him.'

'Yes Jane I know, for it is only an emotion such as that that could make you this unreasonable. You will not leave the gates and everyone who calls upon you is expected to speak to me first. I will not have you foolishly gallivanting about town like a woman with no morals. You may leave.'

Jane was lucky, she had gotten the better part of her father's temper. If it were a situation far more serious he would have already called upon the guards. There would be no telling what he would do to William. She was glad all he had punished her with was time in a house she rarely left. William would now be calling upon her in the presence of her family. An action they had discussed would begin soon. Now it was time to worry about Derek and his new found love.

**

She found Leila looking out the window. Her eyes were wide with astonishment. She must have seen the gardens, 'Don't you have gardens in the America's?'

Leila turned around and smiled. But there was something in her smile that Jane found rather dishonest. 'We don't exactly call home the America's. Derek says that too.'

'What do you call home?'

'We just call it America,' she turned back to the window. Jane was not sure what it was about her but she did not like this woman Derek had brought home. She had a strange way of being. She would wait for a few days, maybe it was because she was in a new environment.

'Derek told me the King has a ball and that is where one meets a prince or the King himself'

'Yes it is, but only mama and papa go to those. They are far too boring to entertain people of our age. We prefer to have our own soiree while they are away.'

She smiled again, 'you don't presume Derek would be willing to go,' there was something amiss with this woman. She would have to ask Derek if his fiancée was still ailing from the journey. Though she seemed rather lucid. 'And of course you and your sister Sarah, who I am yet to meet.'

'Derek is much like me in that way, he and I do not quite enjoy gatherings where society is ready and willing to judge every step you make. We much prefer sitting at home with close friends, I playing the pianoforte while the gents have their talks on business.'

'That is rather boring. He didn't tell me that.'

'It is nothing to tell Leila, that is the English way to be. It is known fact. Even the French with their noses in the air know that.'

She laughed. 'I hope to meet a prince soon. I am sure he would not mind if I asked.'

'You will have to ask after new year. The King already threw his grand ball at the beginning of the season and the next one will be the next season. If you are to be married to my brother you will still be here.'

'Yes,' Leila said with no trace of a smile on her lips, 'if.'

'Good Lord Jane I have been looking everywhere for you,' Derek came bursting through the doors. 'I see you've met Leila.'

'Yes, I certainly have.' Leila had no trace of gladness to be seeing the man she was so in love with she left her home to be with him. Was she with child? Jane's eyes moved to her stomach, but it was flat. There was no evidence of an oncoming bump. Who was this woman, she certainly did not love her brother. She seemed more interested in meeting a prince than focusing on the Duke to be she had. Was her brother still the Duke to be?

'I am glad, I hope you two will get along well," he chose to stand beside Jane.

'Derek may I speak to you for a moment. Do excuse us,' she said to Leila.

**

The conversation with her brother did not go well and Jane found herself twice in one day being reprimanded for things she found absolutely no fault in. her father had been cold towards her and her mother did not want to bring up the subject of William. He had not called upon her in three days. He was wise to stay away, she knew when he finally did come her father would not let him have any peace whatsoever. Derek had escaped their father's temper but his was now directed at her. Leila had began to charm their mother, but Sarah had mentioned she found her strange but settled on her  being from America.

Their father's visitor had arrived and Sarah had not stopped running about looking after him. Charlotte had made herself a constant body in their house and with Charlotte came her brother Matthew. Jane was glad, she had someone to talk to. Matthew was a man who held no judgement and she found herself opening up to him with no hesitation. Even with William there were things she did not mention for fear he would lose his interest in her.

Second Lieutenant Wickam was a rather agreeable man and he sought Jane out every opportunity he got. The ball in London was about to begin and he had insisted the family join him in welcoming the other soldiers before the hunting games. There were times during their conversations he would mention a man, who he seemed to hold a lot of contempt for. This man he spoke of but never mentioned a name had done the unimaginable. He had mentioned more than once he would never have to set his sights on him again.

Wickam seemed like a reasonable forgiving man, she wondered what this man had done to earn himself such an opinion in the eyes of others. He had mentioned a sister, a sister he knew had suffered under the hand of this man.

'It is far too early for one to be sitting here, don't you think?' his voice brought her from her thoughts.

'You forget Wickam this is my house. I am at liberty to walk wherever I please.'

'May I join you?'

'Of course,' she moved to create room for him. She had noticed he and Sarah had begun to spend quite the amount of time in each other's company. More than any other man Sarah had the courtesy of meeting. 'How are you faring Lieutenant?'

'Please, call me Wickam. Lieutenant is for my superiors.'

'Are you saying we are not?'

He smiled, Jane's sense of humour surpassed any he had ever heard and yet the whole of England believed her mute and boring. 'You are not a soldier Lady Jane, only soldiers adhere to ranking.'

'If you insist I call you Wickam, please call me Jane.'

'If the lady insists.'

They sat in silence for a moment but Jane's curiosity would not let her mouth remain silent, 'forgive me for asking, you told me of a man who wronged your sister. What on earth could the man have done that was ever so horrid to her he earned complete hatred from you?'

'Lady Jane,' the voice thundered against the calmness of the morning. Jane jumped a little. She stood up to the face she had been praying to see. He had finally come to see her. Had he spoken to her father? What had her father said? Would this cause William to turn away? There were many questions she was ready to ask him. But her manners preceded her curiosity, Wickam stood up and turned to face William. 'William, I mean Lord William,' she corrected her error. She did not want Wickam to believe her a loose woman. 'This is Second Lieutenant Wickam Charles the third.

William extended his hand and caught Wickams in the air. The handshake was firm. William had had the pleasure of shaking many a soldiers hand but they were never this firm. He looked the man in the eye and gave a small nod of acknowledgment, then turned his focus on Jane.

He missed the storm that brewed in the eyes of the man before him.

# Chapter 17

A new chapter for all you beautiufl people

Thanks for reading and voting...

xoxox.......

Wickam watched Jane and William throughout luncheon. The way they smiled to each other and laughed and when they thought no one was looking their fingers would intertwine. He felt sick. He looked at Jane and how helplessly she looked at William, as if he was the ground she walked on. His decorum and upbringing kept him from throwing the table and giving William exactly what he deserved. Jane was falling in love with a scoundrel who would not think twice about abandoning her and lifting the skirts of the next girl.

He had done it before and cost someone he knew dearly her sanity. Once a rake always a rake is what they would say in the army. He was thankful for the hunting games the Duke threw every year had finally come and there would be much more company for Jane to be in.

He looked over at Sarah who had barely touched her food and smiled. His temper drowned almost as if it had never been there. She was unlike her sister and every bit a young lady who had just come out. She was jittery and smiled a little too much for his liking but there was something about her company that made her appealing in his eyes. She had not inherited the ocean blue depths of her siblings but she was every bit as beautiful as Jane. He had been warned there lived a mute and a perky annoying one in the Duke of Devonshire's home yet all he had met was a timid girl, but every bit intelligent and another enthusiastic for life.

The table was now in a roar of laughter. He had missed the comment and looked about hoping no one would notice he was only smiling. The Duchess had now turned her attention to William, 'Lord William, please tell us more about yourself. It seems Jane is the only one at this table who has any knowledge on you.'

He wiped his mouth with his napkin and smiled, 'there is hardly anything to tell. My mother is French and my father is English. As you can imagine with the state of both the territories, their wedding was not something their families were pleased about. My mother, every bit the devoted wife, moved here to England with my father. They had me shortly after and my sister came, finally. My mother was in fits crying to herself only having had one child. She loves Camille with all her heart.'

'Does that mean you are neglected Lord William? Sarah spoke. She was always one to listen intently on a good story. No doubt Charlotte would be hearing of this one, if she could milk it for all its worth.

'No, Lady Sarah not in the least bit as you can imagine Jasper and I found ourselves with far too much time on our hands.'

'I can only assume there were not enough ladies in society?' she returned. The table silenced and all eyes were now on her. 'I am sorry Lord William, I spoke out of turn.'

'My reputation is the only thing my father holds against me Lady Sarah, please, there is no need to apologize.'

The rest of the conversation was fairly awkward with William answering all the questions sent in his direction. Some of them being a little more personal than he would have preferred but he had to find a way to change the opinion the Duke and the Duchess had of him. Jane had told him they were rather upset with what had occurred between them when they had gone into town and her father expected nothing more than a marriage proposal to transpire. He was more than happy to marry Jane but first he had to take care of Constance. She was still in London wreaking havoc everywhere she went. She had found a number of suitors and no doubt rubbed them in William's face, bringing them to the house he had acquired for her.

He cared very little for what she was doing as long as she kept her adventures discreet as well as her true identity. No one had come to ask him as of yet but he knew it would only be a matter of time before some old hag became far too curious. If Jane found out he was married she would never forgive him. He had told himself Jane was simply a woman of interest and he enjoyed the time he spent in her company. His affections for her grew everyday and he found it harder to say to himself she was simply an adventure.

When luncheon ended the Duke politely asked William to excuse his presence, for the family had business to attend to. William did so with grace and bid farewell to Jane. Wickam, for one, was glad he had left. His father and the Duke were the best of friends. His father had always told him if he ever needed help Duke Weldrake was the one he would turn to and he had offered Wickam the same courtesy. Wickam owed it to the Duke to tell him of the kind of man his daughter would be forever chained to.

**

'Matthew, what an hour to be standing by the pianoforte,' Jane said from the door. She had not seen him for a few days and had missed his presence dearly. Their conversations always seemed to brighten her day. But today he looked rather gloom. His hair was in somewhat of a disarray. 'What on earth is the matter?'

'My sister has finally shamed us all.'

'Come sit,' she made her way to the seatee and extended her hand to Matthew. He looked rather hollow, she noticed now that he was seated next to her. His face was pale and he looked like he had not had much sleep. There was clear evidence of alcohol on his breath. Whatever Charlotte had done had surely driven her brother to the bottle. 'Tell what the problem is Matthew.'

He put his head in his hands and started sobbing. He shook when he felt Jane's hand on his back. He had tried to tell Charlotte it was not worth it, running away for a man she barely knew, but she would not listen. Now the consequences of what she had done would forever haunt their family. The ton would speak it for generations. He had seen this happen to other families.

There were people they were not allowed to associate with because of past faults. Faults, not of their own doing, but those of ghosts past. 'She ran off with some soldier. It was only for three days, I went out to find her. My mother was beside herself with worry and Charlotte did not even care. You do know of the soldiers reputations do you not? They take their liberties with women and when they are done they move on. They will only be in London for a few months. That is surely enough time for them to do what they may.

Charlotte the fool she is, believed he actually loved her. She believed he would retire from the army and live with her in his small village. There was no small village. There was no love. He and his friends,' his words stopped and he cleared his throat.

'She was a fool.'

'Calm down Matthew. I am sure whatever she has done can be fixed.'

'How shall we fix the fact my sister chose to give herself to a rake of a man who has now abandoned her. I found her in London. In an alley, Jane. She was crying. Who knows what those soldiers will say. Shall she now start wearing red to balls, so she could show the men how available she is?'

'It was a childish mistake.'

'Sarah is a child and yet she has not grieved your family.'

'Only because she has not been given the chance. If she had her way she would have already. Please calm down Matthew. How many people know of this?'

'My family and the idiot coachman who took her to London, but who knows what the solider's will say. You know a woman's name from their lips is as good as no marriage prospects.'

'Yes that is true, but you must remember most of these soldier's do not even remember the names of their conquests.'

He laughed, a sarcastic laugh, then he stilled and lifted his head to find Jane there. She was there. She had not judged him like he knew the rest of society would. He had thought of confiding in her but he was afraid her strong opinion would cause her to be like the rest of them but she was the farthest thing from aristocracy. She had understood. 'I was so sure you would judge you.'

'Why would I judge you. It is not your fault Charlotte did what she did. And yes she is not tainted, but if your family are the only ones with the knowledge of this there is no need for anyone to come to know of it. It is simply none of their business.'

'What happens when it is time for a suitor.'

'Then it will be time for a suitor. If the man truly loves her he will understand.'

Jane smiled at him. What he did next was beyond his capability to stop. He grabbed her and kissed her. Jane was too much in shock to respond. He pulled back and ran a hand through his hair. What had he done. He was looking for comfort now he was no better than the man who had taken advantage of his sister. 'Excuse me,' he said and left abruptly.

Jane was left seated alone. Her fingers brushed her lips. She could feel a hot and tingly sensation. Nothing compared to when William had kissed her. She had chosen to give into fate and now it seemed she has received more attention than she had bargained for. She could not move or speak, when Sarah came bursting through the doors screeching something about Wickam, she could not hear what she was saying. She saw her sister and she saw her lips moving but she could not hear, the only sound in her ears was the sound of her heartbeat. It was beating much faster than usual. She tried to think of William but he seemed like a distant memory.

Every image in mind was Matthew. His smile, his laugh. His conversation. Everything was Matthew.

# Chapter 18

---



The men had gathered with their rifles and the horses were being saddled. The Duke was speaking to the men while the women were setting the picnic. They had brought baskets and wine and bread and fruits. It was a Weldrake tradition. Jane remembered being envious of her brother when the men sat atop their horses and disappeared into the woods, coming back hours later with a deer and a look of triumph on their faces. She had begged her father to let her join the men but he had always insisted it was far too dangerous for women. She swore to herself she would prove him wrong. That was the motivation she needed to learn how to ride a horse.

She was now better at it than any of the other men, a much faster rider and a much better shot than any of them it was completely unheard of a woman joining the ride but she was fortunate her father was the Duke.

What he said became the law. If his daughter wished to partake in hunting, she would do so under the watchful eye of her brother.

Derek had thought it would be no fun to babysit his sister while the other men went about riding but he was shocked to see she left him behind. He had now become accustomed to treating his sister like one of the men when they mounted their horses.

Derek had made sure Leila had made herself scarce since her arrival. His father had not spoken to him and his mother looked rather old for a lady of her tender age. Leila had remained adamant about meeting the King or at least a prince and never stopped talking Derek's ear off about why they had to live so far away from life itself. He was gradually getting tired of hearing her rantings and buried himself in work simply to avoid being in her company for the entire day. Before he left the America's she certainly seemed a lot more eager to meet his family and see his estate but now it seemed he did not know her at all.

He had gone to Jane with his concerns and his ever loving sister had asked him to give her time, it was not everyday someone was amongst royalty and the privileged. He was raised in this life and saw it as nothing, yet in her eyes it seemed like they lived almost like Gods. It was understandable. It had laid his doubts to rest, but yet he still preferred to be in the company of anyone but his fiancée.

The Duke made his speech, which surprisingly did not change and the people clapped and the rifle was fired and the horses went. Jane was at the front of the line, her horse disappeared amongst the trees first, and right behind her was Matthew.

**

'You don't suppose I can find my brother about these parts,' Camille interrupted Jasper's thoughts. She had noticed he and William had been spending far too much time in London and whispering amongst themselves. She knew her brother was up to something. The last time he had behaved in this manner he had gone off with some woman. This time she was worried he would drag Jasper with him.

She had known this man all her life and yes she was far younger than he but it was not a scandal for a lady to marry a man twice her age. It happened all the time. The marquis of Canterbury had just taken a wife twenty years his junior and it was far from scandalous. She wondered if he ever saw her in that way. She had often caught him staring, but it was simply because she had a pretty face and had nothing to do with the fact that she was an attractive young lady he could one day marry. It was foolish of her to even harbor these thoughts. She shook her head and focused on finding her brother. She had wished to be at the hunting games this year. Most of the ton attended and she was hoping for a good match at the end of them.

'No, you cannot,' he answered bluntly.

'I was simply asking. I wish to speak to him briefly but I apologize if I have caused you anger by inquiring after my brother,' she crossed her arms over her chest and walked out of the room.

Jasper had not meant to snap at her, he was simply sour after discovering a certain gentleman had been calling on Camille and she seemed to have taken a liking to him. William had mentioned this gentleman more than once and whenever he called upon them she certainly seemed to be in a better mood. She had stopped interrupting their meetings every five minutes and was always moving about with an ink pot and papers.

He had had the chance to court the woman and had decided against it, he did not see the need to be upset. It was his foolish notion that had caused her to show her affections elsewhere. He just wished she would not be so open about them. He went back to his letter. William had requested he pen a letter to an existing relative of Constance's he had fallen upon. She did not know he knew of this distant half brother, they both doubted she knew of his existence herself.

If he could get into contact with Constance it would lift off the burden she was being to William at the moment. She would be far more focused on discovering her new found relative and less intrusive on William's affairs. After this was over and Camille was still unmarried, he would court her and marry her or maybe he would marry her then court her. He was still a little unsure of the order. He had just began to pen his letter when the door opened again and Camille walked in with a tray of tea and biscuits.

She set it down on the desk, 'mama said a man should never be left to attend to his duties on an empty stomach. It is past luncheon and you have not left this room. It is not much but this is all I could steal under the very watchful eye of Cook.'

'Thank you,' he replied keeping his eyes on his current task.

'Is there something bothering you Jasper? You have been quite the sour company and I at least assumed we were friends. Is the manner in which you treat your friends?'

Her utterance shocked him. He looked up at her with shock etched on his face, 'whatever do you mean?'

'You have been banging doors and avoiding me as if I am the plague. Whatever is wrong with you Jasper, I pray you find a solution. You are quite the cranky company and I do not like being put out for something that is not my fault.'

She did not leave the room instead stood her ground and kept her eyes on him. Jasper was at a loss of words. What was he supposed to tell her? He was foolish to not have courted her in the beginning and now she was soon to be attached to another man and he was feeling guilty? 'Nothing is the matter with me, the weather has been a bore that is all.'

'Jasper, I am not one of those loose women you and William spend your days with. I can tell a lie on your face when I see one.'

'We do not all have a husband in waiting Camille,' he blurted out.

'So you are saying you are tired of keeping the secret you are in fact interested in men?'

'What, stop speaking nonsense. Please leave me to continue my work Camille I have no mind to continue this conversation.'

'Fine. Do not come running to me when the rest of the world has turned their back on you because you are queer.' And still she did not move.

'Is there something else you wanted?'

She had turned serious. Jasper sat back, he sure he was going to enjoy her anger. She was always so adorable when she got angry and she had the beautiful ability to wire herself up over the smallest of issues. He just hoped it was something he could handle. 'You and my brother are the best of friends. He says he could never trust someone as much as he trusts you and yet you are the utmost fool. I have batted my eyelids and done all the things necessary to show a man interest and you have completely ignored them. But the second a rumor flies around the walls of this house I am soon to be married you raise a temper. If you have affections for me I pray, tell me now before I accept the hand of a man I can never see myself loving.'

Jasper was speechless. Was Camille coming to him to ask for his hand. This was ever so highly improper. He stopped thinking. Did she just say she had affections for him? 'Pardon me?'

'I would very much like it if you could tell me whether I need to accept the hand of a man whom I do not love as you have taken many a woman to your bed but harbored no emotion towards any of them.'

'Camille.'

'Should I accept the gentleman's proposal?'

'No.'

'Very well. I shall leave you to your tasks. Good day Jasper,' with that she left the room.

Try as he may he was not able to finish the letter.

# Chapter 19

H appy reading....

xoxox.....

'I must admit I have never seen a woman ride a horse as fast as you have today Jane,' Matthew said falling into step with her after he had handed his horse to the stable hand. He had never seen a woman do or say any of the things Jane did or said. She was truly a wonder. He had not meant to kiss her but she was there being everything he wanted in a wife and it just happened. He was sure she resented him because of it. He and Charlotte had been invited, but their mother had forbidden Charlotte to leave her room after what she had done. Matthew was grateful for Derek's friendship, it was because of it he had even considered being a part of the games.

When he had arrived, he avoided Jane, but he knew he would have to face her and he would tell her his feelings. Matthew was sure he would end up alone and unmarried, his father had always said he was far too picky for a man and was once accused of being a queer. But he knew why he was picky. He could not stand women whose priority in life was fashion. It was not always a bed of roses in a marriage he had witnessed that with his parents, but when the time came when love was not always there they had friendship and conversations to depend on and when the love came back they were always stronger than ever. His mother understood him and always encouraged him to find a woman he could talk to and not only love.

She had said marriage was a combination of things and that was what the young did not understand. Matthew was proud of himself, now approaching his later life, at the very mature age of twenty and nine he had no children and no women running after him because of false promises he had made. Like every other man he had had one or two inappropriate meetings but he soon learned his values were not anywhere near those gentleman's clubs. He preferred to be home with a woman he could look at for the rest of his life and he had seen that woman in Jane. She was pure and simple. Sensible and strong yet delicate and believed in a dream. She was what he had been waiting for.

He was sure she was afraid of giving her heart to another after what had transpired in her past but he knew she was a sensible woman and she would be able to tell the difference between a man who wanted her because she was beautiful enough to be wanted and a rake who sought amusement in innocent women. He had watched her ride and was more than impressed with her skill on a horse. He had not imagined meeting her by the river that day would lead him to feelings he was sure would consume him whole. Her hair in its ever present braid was draped over her shoulder and stray hairs flying all about her face. The wind was determined to tangle her neat braid as much as it could. The sun was slowly disappearing behind clouds he was sure would pour buckets of water upon them in no time, but the rays hit her eyes and they shone, ever so bright. He was sure it the excitement she got from riding. Then he wondered how her father ever allowed her to participate in something even the most skilled riders have collected scars and one, he heard, had lost a limb. He was positive his daughters would not ride, they would not participate in anything that posed a threat to their well being. He would not be able to stomach the thought of them in pain.

She was taking off her gloves and her hand slipped from the course material with such delicate care he almost reached out to touch it. 'I have had more than enough practice.'

'It is still beyond me how your father permits you to ride.' She stopped walking and turned to face him. He had awoken her, her eyes became a pool of opinion. She was ready to defend woman kind, but then a voice came from behind them. She turned away from him and she was gone. Her attention was now focused on the man approaching them. The future Duke of Sussex, William.

The rain had come sooner than anyone had anticipated and they had to abandon their meal outside and run for shelter. Jane had spent ample time in William's company since he had arrived. When the rains started he gladly took off his coat and led her indoors before she was wet. They were now seated in the drawing room, her sister was at the pianoforte. She was quite the talented one and her voice was exquisite, nothing like he had ever heard before. If they were not so many rules in society she might have sang in a club where her voice would be appreciated. Unfortunately society was rather cruel to woman who made a living for themselves and he imagined the Duke drew the line with Jane and her riding. That sort of rebellion in a family was only permitted for one child. The Lieutenant was a constant at Sarah's side. He found the man rather agreeable, they had had a conversation or two and the man seemed upright in morals and values and he spoke ever so fondly of the young Lady Weldrake, Matthew was sure a proposal would be the final outcome of his stay.

'Oh come now Matthew, do not stare so hard. You will surely run a hole through my sister,' Derek joined him by the fireplace. He had stood there hoping the crowd in the room would hide him well enough so he could watch her.

'Pardon me, I know it is rude to stare.'

Derek laughed at this response. This is exactly the kind of man his sister needed one who was respectful to the awful laws put in place to make life a terrible bore. 'Please, no pardons needed. It is I who needs to be pardoned, interrupting a man's thoughts is rude, so Janie says.'

'She is quite the rider, how on earth did your father permit her to be.'

'With Janie, there is no permitting or not permitting. She does as she pleases. She has made all of England believe her mute yet she is one of the most difficult people I have ever met. She is far to opinionated and always has something to say about everything. She is judgmental,' Matthew now turned to focus on him, 'yes, she is. Just like our father. She is very proper. But she is also the one responsible for the man I am today. She is harsh with her advises but they are always right. She is objective and perceptive and she loves with all her heart. Do not tell Sarah but she is my favorite sister. She does not like my fiancée, I am starting to believe I made a mistake.'

Matthew was in awe of the description Derek had just given. 'Leila is sweet but she is different, Janie says it is because she is not used to this life, but I can see it her eyes, she too sees something in Leila that she does not like. We have fought far too many a time, I believe she is just trying to spare my feelings.'

'The description you have just given makes me believe otherwise.'

'Janie is complex, Matthew. She will hurt you and love you all at once, by jove, if she was not my sister I would marry the mad woman. Oh come, do not look at me like that my father says the same thing to dear Sarah. This family is rather strange. I do not know who would willfully join it with all this knowledge.'

'The Duke seems rather serious, a man who does not smile in the least, forgive my saying.'

'He assumes that is what a Duke is supposed to be like. I told you my father and Jane are far too similar, marrying her would be equivalent to marrying the Duke himself.'

'Is that so son?' The Duke said approaching them.

'Another thing this family has is exceptional hearing,' he joked. His father and mother stopped by the fireplace.

'The rain surely knows how to spoil a perfect day,' the Duchess commented.

'Not quite mama, you have your three children all matched perfectly. Sarah is by the pianoforte convincing that poor soldier her playing and singing is enough to hold a marriage Jane is with Lord William, no doubt pretending she has no opinion on anything whatsoever, and I have a foreign beauty somewhere about this room. We shall all be married by the new year. A blessing no doubt. Our children will already be matched before they are born for this will be named the family of fortune.'

'Derek,' his mother reprimanded him sharply. 'Please forgive my son,' she looked to Matthew, 'are you not Charlotte's brother?'

'Yes, Your Grace,' this statement earned laughter from the Duke and Derek and a look of scorn from the Duchess. 'Forgive me but have I spoken out of turn?'

'My dear mama seems to think Your Grace is a term of insult. She is not that old, so she likes to believe.'

'Age is just a number dear,' his mother replied. 'A human's true age is in their heart.'

'Of course it mother.'

Matthew watched the playful banter between mother and son and was amazed. There was a lot to the Weldrake family. They seemed to him like a true family, if the title was taken from them they would still be a family, unlike other aristocrats he knew.

'We must not spend too much time here dear, people may think we are being rude in our own home,' the Duchess commented, before she and the Duke went to start up a conversation with another group of people.

'Your family is quite the thing.'

'I told you,' Derek placed his glass of brandy on the plaque of wood above the fireplace and excused himself. He was not blind he could see the admiration in Matthew's for his sister. He had also spoken to Wickam who seemed convinced William was not the man he set himself out to be. Derek would do anything for his sister, but first he had to be sure. She was a well educated lady but there was no education in love and she had learned that the hard way. 'Jane,' he interrupted her and William, who looked the least bit amused. 'May I borrow my sister, I am afraid the matter cannot wait.'

William nodded in approval he did not let her go before he placed a kiss on her ungloved hand. Derek was not one to observe but he noticed Jane pull her hand away much faster than the permitted time for such an action.

'Janie, is there something you would like to tell me?' he asked her as they left the room.

William and Matthew watched them walk out, Matthew with admiration and William simply just watched, but the figure that placed itself next at the door caused him to choke on the sip of brandy he had just taken. She was here. Standing in the doorway of a home she had not been invited to and by her side Lady Maria, his supposed betrothed. William knew he was in trouble. Wickam from the other end of the room followed his gaze and soon enough understood the reason for William's sudden lack of air.

# Chapter 20

 little lengthier, have a great day lovlies...

xoxox...

The atmosphere in the room soon changed. Constance entered the room and the attention she demanded was given to her. Maria was by her side looking terrified of the eyes that had all turned to them. She had met Constance when the soldiers arrived back in London, the lady seemed quite pleasant and a friendship was soon sparked. But Maria had had years of experience and she knew when people were hiding their true agenda's. The minute they walked into the room she came to understand the reason behind her insistence on them making themselves present at the Weldrake home. It was unheard of two unaccompanied women inviting themselves for any sort of event. This would surely run her reputation into the ground. A reputation she already had no hold of. Her mother would not doubt burn her in a fire, for she believed her a witch by now, only one would have no matches after all the balls and soirees she attended.

William looked as handsome as ever and she was unfortunate not have caught his attention. She searched the room for the man she was positive would be here but he was nowhere to be seen. She had heard Derek was unlike other ton members and he cared not for these sort of gatherings. She had however hoped she would at least get a glimpse of him. Constance left her by the door and sauntered off towards William, to cause a scandal no doubt. She remained by the door and moved only when two bodies appeared behind her. She was ready to issue a thousand apologies when she turned and saw who it was. Derek with his sister on his arm. She had not seen the woman he had been with in town and was grateful for that. It would be her turn to turn on a man and make him fall for her charms and a proposal would result from the encounter and soon she would be married and rid of her mother.

What would she do with her mother, put her up in one of those homes that housed widows of the war. Those women had plenty to do, they were allowed to re marry and were not cast out of society. Her mother would complain but the freedom of it would surely be welcome. She always complained of having nothing to do and no one to talk to. There were more than enough women there and she would be at liberty to pick another husband. Marry a man worth her wealth, which was not as much as she made people believe. Maria was curious why her mother had never remarried if her father was such a terrible man. Maybe it was because she was insufferable and no man wanted a woman who complained as much as she did. She would not marry her mother if she were a man. It would be nearly impossible to please the woman. All she ever did was scold her and the household. There was never a happy day in her life. It was sad.

'Pardon me, I did not mean to stand in the doorway.'

Derek seemed to have lost his words for he simply stood there and looked at her. 'Lady Maria is it not,' Jane spoke up with a smile. 'Please it is we who need to apologize. Just because it is our home does not mean we can walk however we want. Are you here with company?'

'Yes, Lady Constance, she is an acquaintance of Lord William's. We just recently befriended one another.'

Jane squeezed Derek's arm a little, this brought him back to the present, 'Welcome,' he took her hand and kissed it lightly. For some reason he wished there was music to accompany this excursion. Sarah's playing was impeccable but it was not danceable in the least. And many of the guests had abandoned their usual attire for riding clothes which offered, again, no room for dance. It would be rather scandalous watching a woman in breeches dance. His father would never hear of it. Jane excused herself and gave him a stern look. He knew his duty as an owner of the household. He knew how to be hospitable. When he had met Maria in the shop she had certainly not looked this beautiful. Her face held a fatigue he imagined came from a long day inside a coach. She also looked much older than she did as she stood in front of him in this moment. He was sure they had met an entirely different woman but she responded to Jane's queries which could only mean, she was the same woman.

'Lord Derek, are you alright?' Maria asked. He had stood there far too long not making any movement whatsoever.

'Yes I am,' he regained his senses, 'please,' he offered her his hand so they could walk in together. The room again turned on them as they entered and a few murmurs were heard. Jane had placed herself by William's side once again and Constance was too standing by William. Wickam had kept his distance but there was no doubting the anger in his eyes at the sight of Constance or maybe it was William. He had been very vocal to Derek of the dislike he harbored for William. He found it misplaced for Derek had believed Wickam had affections for his other sister. Matthew was still by the fireplace and on his fifth glass on Brandy. The man could hold his liquor, in Derek's opinion that was a man that had been jilted once and sought solitude in a bottle to the point it had no effect on him. His eyes were still firmly placed on Jane and she would turn once or twice and steal a glance of her own.

Constance had insisted on having a conversation that required a lot of physical contact with William. He found this quite odd and the way she laughed was clear she knew the man, well. Maria had said she was an acquaintance of his, it was normal, probably a distant cousin.

Derek led Maria to a chair and offered to fetch her a drink but she declined. She had had enough drink in the company of Constance she believed she would soon have an addiction. Derek sat down beside her, 'it is a great pleasure seeing you again Lady Maria.'

'I see your sister did quite the work with your attire, if I may be so bold to say. You look less ragged.'

'Yes, well it is hard to dispute Jane's taste. It is she who has kept me clothed.'

'Do not let your mother hear you. She may put you over her knee.' He laughed. She was funny. A quality he had overestimated in Leila. Why was he comparing his fiancée to this woman?

'It is unfortunate I missed the riding. I am sure I would have out ridden a good number of you men.'

'It is unlikely, Lady Maria. This is a family of riders and those not from the family have participated in the hunting games far longer than you have been alive.'

'Pardon me, but how old do you think I am?'

'No greater than twenty and one of course. You are but a child.' Maria laughed. She had never so complimented in her life. With her well made face and constant red lips she knew she looked far older than she was, but without it she was sure she fit her age quite well. 'have I misjudged your age?'

'Greatly Lord Derek, now I shall put the task of finding out my true age on you. For my lips shall never speak it.' This statement drew his attention to them. They were plain, clear of any rouge or even a slight dab of pink. She was beautiful. He straightened and pulled his eyes back on hers.

'Lady Maria, full of surprises aren't we? I must tell you I have a great advantage over you.'

'Yes, and what is your advantage?'

'My sister by the pianoforte I believe knows every man, woman and child in England. I will have your age by the end of the day.'

'When you do have it, please make sure you seek me out,' with that she stood and went to seek the company of an older man perhaps. One she did not feel the ever growing need to be in the company of. He was with another, she was sure. She would not be the one to break a promise already made, no matter how forward this man was. It was pure bliss being in his company but if he wanted to be in hers he would find her when he discovered her age. Only a man interested would seek her out.

**

Jane was not quite sure she understood the conversation going on between Constance and William. It seemed far too intimate but not intimate enough. Constance made sure to touch William's hand with every comment and barely spoke to her. Jane was sure he would still speak to her parents and offer for her hand. They had spent most of the day discussing it. They had already picked a perfect location for their wedding to take place and they had agreed they would reside near her parents. Jane could not imagine not seeing them at least once a week. And Derek, he would no doubt not be able to survive without her. He could marry any girl. Leila had made herself scarce during this gathering. They had found her in her room seated by the window still inquiring if a Prince would attend and she seemed uninterested to join them when Jane had told her there would be no Prince present.

Derek was surely the dumbest man she had ever met. His choice in women seemed to be getting worse. She stole another glance at Matthew and again she found his eyes still on her. He did not turn away when their eyes met, he only nodded and went back to staring. She was beginning to feel every bit uncomfortable. She looked between William and Constance, they were still deep in their conversation regarding an unsettled issue between them. She remembered what it felt like to be kissed by him but it was a far and very distant memory yet it had happened twice. Her mind was full of Matthew's and the effect it had had on her. She had not been able to sleep. Whenever she would close her eyes his image filled her mind.

It was becoming impossible to be close to him but she told herself it was simply because she spent a considerable amount of time in his company it was only natural she found herself drawn to him. She hoped that was all it was. She would not marry a man when she was holing affections for another. She had to speak to him, maybe he did not intend to kiss her and it was a mistake. She felt her heart drop at the thought it might have been a mistake. She turned her attention back to Constance and William. Her eyes were trained on Jane with so much anger and hatred. Jane felt she had missed a rather heated conversation, the room had suddenly become very quiet and everyone was now watching them. She looked back at Matthew and his face spoke pure rage. 'This is the girl you have been parading around town I see,' Constance spoke. Jane turned her attention back to her. 'Dear girl, this man will destroy you like he destroyed me.'

'Pardon me ma'am.'

'Pardon indeed. Congratulations are in order, William tells me the both of you will be married in a month's time. Don't you think that a little soon William?' she turned to him. Why was she calling him William? Did she have no respect for the man standing before her? Even if they were acquaintances, they were in public.

'Constance,' he spoke trying not to raise his voice, 'this is not the place nor the time.

The door opened then and a housemaid walked in and handed Wickam a letter before pardoning herself. The door shut and the attention was back on William, his wife and his wife to be.

'Little girl, let me train on you on all things William, he will say he loves you, he loved me too, did you not? He will say he needs you, there was a time he could not live without me. Look at me now. I am merely a memory, much like his time in the army,' she turned to Jane and looked her over, then spoke with a voice loud enough to draw the attention of everyone in the room, 'you are with child that is why he wants to marry you suddenly is it not? William would never pledge his heart to a woman let alone his entire lifetime.'

The whole room gasped in unison. Jane shook her head and tried to deny the claims but no words could come out of her mouth. She was sure she was not. She was as pure as the day she was born, except a little kiss, she was still intact. How dare this woman come into her house and accuse her this way. She would have defended herself but the eyes that were now focused on her and her stomach were too much. She could not speak, she could not move. She stayed rooted to the spot she was standing. She did not even notice William take Constance by the hand and lead her out of the room nor did she notice Matthew deposit his glass on a tray and leave the room.

# Chapter 21

The room cleared out one body at a time till it was just Jane, her parents, Sarah, Wickam and Derek, all with looks of shock, except her father, he was furious. She had finally done it, she had shamed her family and she had done it in front of her father's prized society. No doubt the rumors would start spreading, all it took was one woman. She was ruined. She had to marry William if she was with child, and even if she wasn't she still had to marry him because they all thought she was with child. Wasn't that what she wanted? He was to speak to her father and ask for her hand. This is what she wanted. If it was truly what she wanted why did she feel so unsure? Why did she feel like she was betraying a soul? Why did she feel like she betraying Matthew?

Suddenly Jane became very aware of her situation. 'So this is the disgrace you can bring down on this family Jane? This is what you are so silent for?' her father's voice came thundering down. He was angry and she knew. Who was this woman William had brought to their home? Why would she think Jane was pregnant? Why would she announce it with such volume? Was she looking to embarrass William?

'Father calm down,' Derek spoke with voice of authority. They rarely heard it, it was reserved for his business. He had never used it on the family, but now he was about to stand up to his father.

'Stay out of this Derek.'

'I am sure Jane can explain to us who that woman is?'

'I do not care for her explanations? You are not to leave your room, are we clear?'

Jane could not speak, the shock of it all had turned her mute. All she saw was her father's rage. He did not have to banish her away, she would not leave her room out of her own will. She knew now what was to come, but her mind was stuck on Matthew, she had not even seen him leave the room. What was he thinking of her? Why had he kissed her? She remembered what it felt like and her stomach turned. Suddenly she felt hot like she could not breath. The room began to spin and she swayed along with the motion. He surely hated her now, he must think her a hypocrite. All the conversations they had, the room stopped spinning. Was she in love with Matthew? It was not possible, William held her heart. They had began talking of marriage, she would not love another man wile planning on marrying another. She had to find Matthew, she had to find out why he kissed her and explain she was not with child. She had to make him understand.

Jane ran from the room, hoping Matthew had not left. He had spoken of riding out after the rains. The sun was barely out but it was enough for one to steal a few moments alone on a horse. It was what she would have done. She ran to stable as fast as her legs could carry her and she was thankful she was right. He was there, he was saddling the horse he had ridden earlier. The force in which he pulled the straps only told her how angry he was. Here she was plain Jane, running after a man. It was a spectacle for sure. 'Matthew,' she said out of breath. She kept her distance in case he ran. She wanted him to stand and listen, he did not have to respond he just had to listen.

Matthew kept pulling at the straps of the saddle.

'Matthew, please,' she did not want to beg but she knew she had to. She did not know why it was so important to her he know she was not with child, it could not possibly be love, but she needed him to know.

'I will take my leave tomorrow,' he pulled on the last strap and mounted the horse.'

Jane felt desperation fill up in her, so she did the only thing she knew would keep the horse from moving, she jumped at the reins and held onto them with all the force her body had. The horse moved around trying break free of her hold on it. The more it moved, the stronger she held onto it. 'Matthew please listen to me.'

He jumped off his horse and held onto the reins making sure his fingers do not brush against Jane's, because then he knew he would lose all reason.

'I am not with child.'

'But you plan to marry William?'

She had no response to this statement. She knew she had to marry William but standing here looking at Matthew, she couldn't.

'Your silence speaks volumes young Lady Weldrake.'

'Why did you kiss me?' she had to ask, she had to know.

'The kiss meant nothing Lady Weldrake. I was upset and you were there. I needed to calm my nerves.'

'Matthew,' she gasped. What did he mean it meant nothing?

'You are with child Lady Weldrake, I suggest you turn you attentions to your child and your husband.' He saw the shock on her face. She was hurt and she would hate him but it was what had to be. Whether or not she was with child, her reputation was now ruined. Marrying her would not protect her.

'It was not nothing for me.'

'I am a man Lady Weldrake, we take what we want when we want it. I am afraid that is the truth.'

'You do not mean these words. You are simply trying to hurt me,' tears had started forming in her eyes. Why today of all days?

'Lady Weldrake, I suggest you compose yourself. You are acting untoward. Let go of the reins so I may take my leave.'

She let go of the reins and watched him mount the horse once more and ride off. The kiss had meant nothing to him? So why had he stayed? What was he after? She felt her heart shatter into a million pieces. How could she not have seen it? The thrill of being in William's company was nothing compared to the peace, comfort and safety she felt in Matthew'. How could she have been so blind as not see she did not harbor any feelings for William? That first night they met when he had kissed her hand, she had felt joyous, but only because of the mystery of their surroundings.

The tears fell from her eyes and  bits of her soul leaving her. She felt empty and alone. It was cold and she was alone. Jane did not know how long she stood there watching the path on which Matthew and his horse had disappeared, but it was now dark and she felt a warm hand on her shoulder. She could not tell who it was, she was not sure she cared to know. All she wanted was Matthew to ride back and tell her he was sorry and he understood. He did not give her the opportunity to explain, he did not want to listen. She knew she would not see him again. Their last meeting had been one of pain and torture.

'Jane,' William's voice washed over. She was angry. This was his fault. Him and that woman, his supposed acquaintance. 'You have been out here for long. The sun had long set, you will catch an illness in this cold weather.'

'Who was that woman William and why does she think I am with child?' she did not turn around, she was waiting for the sound of hooves riding back.

'Come let's go inside.'

She shook off his hand and turned to walk past him. She would speak to anyone until she spoke to Matthew. Her father wanted her locked away, the shame was too great for him to bear. She would grant his wish. She would hide away and speak to no one and when the time came to marry. She would marry William and remain silent all of her days.

The world thought her mute, she would confirm that one fact.

# Chapter 22

------------------------------

E xtra length, extra crispy

thanks for reading and voting..

xoxox.....

It had been days since anyone had seen or even heard Jane. She remained behind closed doors. Her lady's maid had informed the Duke she was barely eating and spent all her time by the window. She only moved when it was time for her to take her bath. The Duke had now become concerned for his daughter. He had thought Jane was far smarter than this. How could she be with child and refuse to nourish her body. She had to understand she was now taking care of not only herself.

'What has become of our children? I expect this behaviour from Sarah, yet she is the only one going about this the proper way. In full view of us, we can see the courtship.' He was pacing his study and his wife's irritation was growing with every step he took. Her husband had been so angry she had not had a way of informing him she is woman and would know if Jane was with child. She had three of her own and had been a midwife to both her sisters. Her daughter was not with child.

'And Derek and that mute fiancée of his. She does not speak, she does not dine with us, she does not speak to us. Sarah who does not have much intuition about people says she finds her rather strange. Where did we go wrong dear? What have we done to our children that they repay us with a fate so painful?'

'John, please sit down, you are giving me a headache with your pacing,' his wife patted the space beside her. The Duke played with her suggestion in his mind before setting himself down beside her. 'Jane is no more with child than I am, and I am telling you that was a woman who has borne three children of her own and a few more of her sisters. Whoever that woman was, she was simply trying to cause shame and not for our daughter, but for the man our daughter has been in the company of.'

'All of England is talking. No doubt the King has gotten wind of this.'

'The King only cares you are performing your tasks and not allying with our enemies. He has no care for your daughter's marriage potential.'

'How on earth will Sarah find a good match?'

'I believe she already has and Derek may not have had quite the sense when he was away, but I believe a certain lady has caught his attention. He will marry well you should not doubt that.'

'And Jane? What of our other daughter? She will be a spinster living in this house and taking care of us when we are old. When we die she will be at the mercy of Derek and his wife. If the woman wants nothing to do with her, where will she go? Become a governess to a family?'

'John,' she placed her hands over his, 'you have such little faith in the man you are. You raised three wonderful children. You must however remember they are but children, not much older than the other. They compete on who will upset us the most they will make mistakes, but we are their parents, we have to be there for them, good or bad.'

'You are not a Duke dear. You do not have to see the faces of the men in the courts as they sit there and judge me silently.'

'I am a mother,' she replied with anger, 'and that is far greater a responsibility than yours. You think I am happy? Do you not think it pains me to see my children as such? We are living in a different time John, one day there may be not decorum to follow and children will do as they please. I am asking you as your wife to not be so harsh on Jane. She only speaks and confides in you and you are the one reprimanding her the hardest.'

'I cannot bring myself to speak to her, I am sorry.'

The Duchess rose to her feet and straightened her gown, 'then there is nothing more you and I have to say to each other.' She left her husband in his study to ponder on her words. She had known men were fools but she never expected her husband to be one of them. She would try to talk to Jane. William had called on them but her husband had refused to give him audience. He had insisted the only conversation to be had was after Jane was safe in her matrimonial home, safe from the prying eyes of the ton.

Why didn't her daughter defend herself when she knew what was being said of her was a lie? She knocked on the door and heard only silence. She pushed it open and saw Jane by the window. She didn't turn when she heard the door nor did she move when her mother put her hand on her shoulder. 'It is a bright day Jane, why not take a walk about the gardens?'

'Papa forbade me from leaving this room or speaking to a soul until William and I are married. I am bound.'

'No you are not. This is your home.'

'These are walls in which I reside in mama, there is no home here.'

'Talk to me dear,' she turned her around and gasped. Jane's eyes were red and swollen. Her cheek bones were more pronounced and the colour of face was evident she had not slept or eaten. 'What on earth?' There was no expression that could mouth the shock etched on the Duchess' face, 'you will surely wither away Jane, no one can marry a corpse.'

'No one will marry me mama, whether or not I am a corpse.'

'Be quiet, do not speak such evils. I know you are not with child and your father is upset, but when h cools down I promise he will see reason. Derek and Sarah have been asking after you and Wickam had been pleading to remove you from here so he may speak with you. I will not let you sit here in self pity when there is an army of people who can take care of you.'

Jane laughed. An army? There were only a handful of people her mother had mentioned. She was sure even if she wrote him, he would no sooner send her letter into the fire. Matthew had left the next day as he promised and she had not heard of him. Sarah had sat outside her door on occasion and given her gossip but none of it was of Matthew and she did not care to of it.

The woman that had caused her shame was still a mystery and try as they may the ton did not know who she was to William and why she had been so outspoken and much less at a gathering she was not invited to. Sarah rested on the assumption she was a woman William had jilted in the past and was only looking to settle a score with the man. She had disappeared from any prying eyes in London. She was now more of a myth than an actual woman. Derek had also attempted to remove her from her solitude by informing her of his supposed fiancée's departure, she had secured a passage back to the America's. She had said she was bored of the English ways, her want and need to meet a prince had finally driven her back home. A fact Derek came to discover was her only motive of accepting his proposal. She was under the notion she would meet a prince and then leave Derek and become the next Queen of England. He found it silly more than hurtful, the perception of what England was. She had not expected to be locked away in the country away from any true royalty. A lowly Duchess was not what she had planned for herself.

He was now rather taken by the lady they had met in the shop in London when he had first arrived. He informed Jane he sought her out after that fateful day and she was more than a surprise. Her only mark was her family was without finances and she had no fortune to her name whatsoever. She had once had a need to be married to be rid of her mother but now she only truly wanted to marry for love. She happy for her brother, he had found someone more agreeable to court. No doubt he and Sarah would be married before her.

She was happy for her brother and sister, she was happy they had found happiness, maybe if she was more like them she would have been happy too, married maybe. She had her first season a long time ago, she would have spoken a little louder or danced more, she would have gotten a husband. One who may disregard her but a husband nonetheless. It did matter to her that the man she would eventually wed should love her and her only, but now if she was offered for by a man twice her age, her father would certainly see to it she accepts the man's hand. This was now her life. She had to bear the burden the Lady Constance had placed on her shoulders and she had to bear the loss f a friend ever so dear.

How could she not have seen it? She would wait for Matthew to call on them and if Charlotte appeared alone she was always disappointed. She greatly enjoyed the time they would spend together and she would tell him anything and everything. He would never judge her and she never judged him. Even when he told her of the time he and his friend played a cruel prank on their mothers lady's maid. She never harbored any ill feelings towards him. She should have known after the kiss, she could think of nothing but him, try as she may she only saw Matthew. William was becoming more like a stranger to her. She did not wish for his company or his comfort. He had called upon her but not to discuss a wedding, why had he not spoken to her father? She was awaiting the time she would be bound to the man for all eternity. Would she have t deal with Constance? The woman seemed like she was on a mission of vengeance. Jane looked at her mother's heartbroken face, but she could not bring herself to care for what her mother was feeling. She had her own emotions to worry over. Her heart was broken, shattered into a million pieces and she saw a future with no hope of it ever being mended.

**

Wickam read the letter again, it was penned to him and upon missing him in London was forwarded, as per his instruction, to Devonshire. He could not believe another knew of his relation to Constance. He had thought he had kept the secret safe with him. The only other man who knew had died in his arms during the war. Who was this Jasper, that was the only sign on the note.

He paced his room with the letter in his hand, why had Constance come out the way she did? Did she have no care for another woman, she was not the woman he had seen all those years ago and she certainly was not the woman he had been reading about in the letters her maid had been sending. He had always thought she was a young, beautiful humble lady, not the wicked one that had resented herself in manner so unladylike and speaking so very out of turn. She had cost Jane her happiness. He too had seen it, she had spent far greater time in the company of the gentleman Matthew than she did with William, who would, as it seems, only call on Jane when he was looking for an adventure. He should talk to her father and expose the man for who he truly was. But if he did they would surely judge him for not speaking as soon as he laid eyes on William and Sarah, dear Sarah would never forgive him for letting her sister continue accommodating a man so vile.

He was at a predicament, he knew what he would do, he would ride to London and confront this Jasper, he needed to find the relationship between him and his sister. Then he could put this matter to rest.

**

'What on earth were you thinking?' William threw the glass in his hand into the fireplace. The flames burned a little brighter with the introduction of brandy. Constance remained seated but straightened her back a little more. She was now afraid. She had never seen William this furious. She knew she had made a mistake of doing what she did but she was not going to stand by and let another woman take claim to what he had promised her. She had learnt of her relation with Matthew and had hoped suspicion that the child may be his would arise giving her the opportunity to further convince William the rumors were true, but it had not worked in her favor.

She had only heard the future Duke of Sussex had struck again. A rake no doubt, the women called him. Many were rather pleased with current situation and a few cried for the loss of an agreeable man. They would have to go seasons without him on the marriage mart. How foolish were the ton? Now she had to deal with the wrath of the man, the one thing she had never been able to tame in him.

'Come now William, calm down. It very unbecoming of a Duke to lose his temper, did your father not teach you that?' she tried to speak in the calmest voice, but this did nothing but anger William further. He took two strides and lifted her from the chair and shook her. Her perfect bun atop her head came undone and now her hair was raging about her face. She was lost in the confusion and pain of it all. The more she screamed the firmer the grasp William had on her. She was sure was going to kill her, but then he let go and ran a hand through his hair. She rubbed her arms ad glared at him. That was when he struck. This was the William she remembered. This was the man she had met all those years ago, he was as sweet as he was poisonous. She had not left because of the promise he had made to her and she would not leave now because she was closer than ever. She would finally live the life her sister had lived and know what it felt like to have everything you ever wanted. It did not matter the man who provided her with it was an animal. She would find comfort in shopping and socializing. She would rub shoulders with the cream of society and who knew she may just meet the King himself someday and find favor in the Queen. All she had to do was be patient, be very patient. William had always thought he had the upper hand, but she had something that would crush his spirit and rid him of his soul. She had something that would destroy him, but she would only use it if it was utmost necessary. Not a moment before.

She landed on the floor with a thud. Her cheek stung, she looked up at the man standing above her, his rage had subsided but his breathing let her know he was not done. She placed her hand on her cheek and readied her body for any more that was coming her way, then there was knock on the door. Constance was part grateful and part frightened, she knew if he did not finish what he started now, he would find time to do it later, he always did. He pulled her off the ground and pushed her into the chair. 'Fix your hair, and look presentable, I would not want people to know I do not tolerate stupidity,' he waited until she was presentable before he moved to the door.

The voice that came in through the small opening William had allowed sent waves of relief through her. It was the soldier from Devonshire. It was rude to turn a soldier away. William would have to see him. She had the length of their conversation to re claim her territory.

g

# Chapter 23

----------------------------------------------------------------

Two chapters, one night

happy reading

xoxox...

William let the man in and motioned for Constance to stay where she was. Wickam sat opposite her and immediately noticed the fear etched on her face. She was doing an impeccable job at covering her right cheek, but was a soldier he knew a wounded man when he saw one. This only infuriated him further. How dare this man do what he did to her and further his torture by beating her. This made hi wonder if William had beaten the child out of her? He would make sure there was nothing left to this man by the time he was done with the conversation they were soon about to have.

'How can I help you?' William straightened his frame and placed himself in his father's seat. A seat that would be his and Jane would be close by. Constance had known what great favor she had done him. All of England thought the child was his, a marriage was inevitable. He would be rid of her and she would have no grounds to make any complaints. He would be the Duke and she would be just a woman scorned.

'The matter I wish to discuss with you is delicate I would prefer to do it in private.'

'She is staying Wickam,' William said bored. This was the soldier who was residing with them. Had he come to ensure he marry Jane. They did not have to force his hand. Wickam only acknowledged Constance before placing the piece of paper on the desk in front of William.

'I believe that was sent to me, I received it the day Constance made her appearance,' William recognized the paper, it bore their royal seal. He opened it and true as day Jasper's name was signed at the bottom. This was the letter Jasper had written to the half brother they heard about. how on earth had Wickam gotten this letter? Was he spy for Devonshire? '

'Tell how you came to be in possession of this letter, are you a spy?'

'No,' Wickam spoke calmly. He looked to Constance who seemed curious as to the contents of the letter, 'I am the brother you addressed the letter to. I asked the boarding house to forward any mail bearing my name to Devonshire. This woman here, is my sister.'

Both William and Constance opened their mouths in shock.

'Nonsense. Your days in the military have ruined your head. I demand you take your leave. I have no time for this foolishness.'

'I did not think you would believe me. Maybe if I showed you how much I know you would be more inclined to believe I am who say I am,' he sat back in the chair. Constance looked between the two men but said nothing. 'The child to demanded she be rid of, or perhaps you would like me start somewhere far more friendly?'

The look of shock was replaced by pure fear on William's face. This man knew of his truths? 'How is it possible you now of these things. Constance has no family to speak of.'

'Her father is my father, he and my mother had an affair, a fact I am not proud of but I am the result. I was asked to make sure my sister is taken care of and she does not end up selling her body for gifts to men who would do no more than use her and toss her out. I was asked not let her become like her sister.'

'You know my sister?' Constance spoke but her words were close to a whisper. She had forgotten William was in the room, she had forgotten she was in fear only moments ago.

'No, I knew of Arabella, your father sent me a very detailed letter before he died. I received it a good year after his death.'

Tears filled her eyes, 'my father,' she stopped

'Forgive me, I thought you knew.'

'Stop this,' William yelled. 'If you are who you say you are why are we only hearing of this now?'

'I have kept my distance as her father asked me, but when I got wind of you I decided to stay a little closer and I was right to. But I am afraid I am far too late to offer her any kind of protection against men like you.'

'I am a Duke.'

'Your father is a Duke, you are simply a child with far too much time and fortune.'

'You will not speak to me with disrespect,' he slammed his fist on the desk.'

'And you will not set another foot at Devonshire. You leave Jane to be. You have caused her too much pain and you are not even wed.'

'Jane is not your concern.'

'She is like family to me.'

William laughed, 'So you want both sisters for yourself. They always said soldiers had no shame.'

'You will treat me with respect William. I and a Lieutenant in the army,' he was now on his feet.'

'And that means nothing to me.' William countered. He would not let this man threaten him in his own home.

'Perhaps his majesty's confident might.'

William had no response.

'Stop it both of you,' Constance rose to her feet. 'Is father truly dead?'

Wickam took a deep breath before nodding his head but keeping his eyes on William, who seemed to have lost the fight in him.

'Where is he buried?'

Wickam was at a loss of words. She did not know the faring of her family. Had she not written letters or visited once or maybe twice. 'There was no body to bury Constance. He had fallen terribly ill and was on his way to London to seek out a doctor when the carriage he was riding in crashed. The passengers were never recovered.'

She gasped and covered her mouth. Her father was gone and she did not even know. She had turned her back on her family all for what? She had only gained material things. Yes she wanted to be the Duchess and it meant it would cost her love but she had never known love. She had never truly been loved and loved deeply, what use would she have for it now? It was William's fault. He had kept her locked away, she had nowhere to go. She was with him and only him and when he was gone she had a lady's maid who was as mute as a cow. She spoke no words. She would tend to her duties and follow Constance but offered nothing in companionship. Is this what her sister had lived like? She had lived like a princess but foregone any kind of compassion or feeling? Is this what it felt like to have everything? Empty?

'What about mother?'

'I am afraid I do not know.'

'So he was never buried? My mother has grieved him and not had the painful comfort of laying him to rest?'

Wickam reached out for her but she took a step back, she was still in pain and did not want the man to notice. He was under the obligation to protect. He would drag William out by his hair and have him branded a woman beater. It would not be a bad thing but she had a goal in sight.

She let one tear fall, that was all the mourning she would do for her father. One tear. She would do all she could to e the daughter he wanted her to be now. She looked at William, he looked deflated and defeated.

'I am leaving with my sister.'

'You will do no such thing,' William tried one last attempt against the Lieutenant.

'I am not going,' Constance spoke.

'Why would you stay with man after what he did to you after what he has done to you?'

'I am not going anywhere Lieutenant.'

'Constance,' he reached for her again.'

'Please respect my wishes Lieutenant. I have only learnt of you today, I know you not and I appreciate your care but I have been on my own for many years, I can assure protection is the one thing I do not need from any man.'

Wickam looked between the two. William was smiling. He would let them be, for now. 'I will respect your wishes.'

'I only ask you write me so I may begin to know you and maybe you can relay to me the details of my father's passing more. I wish to grieve him but I can do that only after I have come to terms with what befell him.'

'Very well,' Wickam did not try to reach for her. He knew she did not want him to see her wounds. He left without bidding farewell to William. As the door closed William turned to Constance. She was standing still, her eyes on the floor. She had caused him far more trouble than he wanted. He would not be able to keep the Lieutenant silent. He was sure the wretched man was on his way to Devonshire to relay the information he had. William was ruined. His father would disown him and he would receive no fortune. His only option was to arrange for a wedding with Jane as fast as he could. He would pen a letter to the Duke, no he would ride to Devonshire himself. The Lieutenant would not run back in haste, William could ride through the night and be there before him. He would arrive after the matter would have already be settled. He would leave immediately. Constance would have to wait for another day.

He would look forward to it.

******

Matthew had barely spoken. He went about his business in complete silence. He had heard of the announcement placed of William's impending marriage. His mother had commented far to openly on her relief he would leave the poor girl destitute even if her father had a substantial amount of money. The rumors of her apparent child had quieted down. Women who had had children of their own confirmed she was not with child but some, for the sake of conversation, had insisted she was simply doing an impeccable job at hiding it.

He had grown tired of the never ending topic and was in desperate need of time to himself. He needed time to mourn the love he lost. He should have stayed after he kissed her, he should have told her then and there he was in love with her. He should have told her he waited his whole life to feel the way he felt but instead he ran. Of course she had been kissed by men, she must have thought it meant nothing. And if she did he only confirmed it to her. Why had he spoken so harshly? Why hadn't he listened to her. He listened on every other occasion why had he chosen not to listen to her then? He was a fool and now he was suffering for it. What was the difference between him and his sister? She was foolish enough to follow her heart and he was foolish enough to not follow his.

She was would soon become the future Duchess of Sussex and he would be Matthew. A man with no woman to love. A man who could have had a woman to love but was far to blinded by anger to let her explain. She had ran after him, if she ran he should have listened. He missed her smile and her laugh and her conversations. He had not had a chance to sketch her, he had wanted to but she had always insisted she was not ready. She was never ready because she did not know the beauty she possessed. Those beautiful blue eyes that changed color depending on her emotions. He had seen them all. He had mastered her heart through her eyes. That day in the stable she was breaking and he was too angry to notice. He was too far gone to stop and do what he had always done, comfort her.

He pulled on his riding boots, maybe a little wind in face would help him relax and possibly lessen the pain on his heart. He was careful not make any noise as he descended the stairs and walked out the door. The stable was a few meters from where he stood. He took in the fresh air and was letting out a breath when he saw a carriage approaching. It bore the symbol of Devonshire. For a moment he was happy, she had come to ask him forgiveness again. This time round he would not let her speak, he would take her in his arms and tell her he understood and he was the one that was sorry for not believing her when she said she was not with child and for behaving like a boy instead of the man she told him he was.

The carriage stopped and a woman descended but not the woman he was expecting. Had she come to deliver a wedding invitation? She did not expect him to attend did she? Despite his words she must know of his feelings towards her.'

'Good day Lord Matthew,' Sarah spoke. She did not know why Wickam had insisted she deliver this invitation personally and did not leave until he agreed on attending. She was lost in all honesty on the going on's in her household. Her father had spent many hours behind closed doors with Wickam and her mother was constantly crying and begging for forgiveness. William too had come and spoken to her father and they he had agreed on a marriage based on the circumstance his dear friend had put Jane in. Jane had continued her silence and Derek had not a kind word to speak of William. She was sorely confused. She and Wickam she believed had grown rather fond of each other and he told her of all his plans except this one. She was to make sure Matthew accept the invitation she held in her hand.

'Lady Sarah,' he said disappointed.

'You seem disappointed to see me. It is not I who vexed you,' Sarah had never learned to spare the feelings of a man. She spoke ever so bluntly and it had served her well with Wickam for he valued honest above all else.

'I apologize. I was under the impression Lady Jane was in the carriage.'

'My sister has not spoken a word since that fateful day. When she does speak her words are drowned in her tears. She speaks of you and how you did not have a care for what she had to say. She is purely convinced you want nothing to do with her.'

'I beg your pardon.'

'Yes Matthew, if I may call you Matthew,' she did not wait for a response, 'Janie is quite taken with you but since you did nothing but scold her and take off what other option does she have but marry that insufferable man who spends time with less than ladylike women. I must say I was surprised myself. But if you were to speak to her she may withdraw her consent.'

'Your father has already placed an announcement.'

'Oh please, if Janie decides she does not want to marry there will be no wedding. She is not with child and is not bound to that man in any way, everybody knows that. Do you not live in England?' she asked.

'Pardon me?'

'Oh yes, Charlotte is under lock and key that is why you know nothing. Let me make I my duty to inform you my sister is not with child and she is in fact still as pure as the day she was born, save for that kiss you gave her, how completely cunning of you to use Charlotte's predicament to further your own agenda.' Matthew was confused. Had Sarah come to scold him for running off on her sister? Had she said Jane was taken with him? Was she still waiting?

'William had to sit with my father three whole times, before he was given permission to marry Jane and that is still to be decided, if Jane does not leave her room there will be no wedding at all. In any case, I was asked to deliver this invitation to you. Please be sure to attend or I will never be allowed to go anywhere on my own. I have delivered five of these and have been told to go home and stop arranging balls without my mother's

permission. Can you imagine the shock on her face when no one arrives.'
She handed him the invitation and gave him a smile before disappearing
back into the carriage. He turned the invitation over in his hand and out
slipped a piece of paper. He waited for the carriage to be a fair distance
before picking it from the ground. It read,

Dearest Matthew,

I know I have caused you nothing but pain and for that I apologize. I was
under the impression you saw me only as a friend and pleasant company
until the day you showed me you care for me more than that. I admit, I too
was too blind to see my feelings towards you were growing each passing
day.

I assume since I have not seen you, you are still angry with me, I want you
to know I understand. My decision to marry William is not my own. Sarah
only told me of the announcement today morning.

I hope one day you will find it in your heart to forgive me for the hurt I
have caused you. I would like you to know my heart is not well in condition
either.

Love Always,

Janie.

He folded the letter in his hand and felt his heart soar. Her heart was not
well in condition, it could only mean she too was feeling like he was.

He opened the invitation, in two days time Jane would be his again, if only
he could convince her forgive him for acting the way he did.

(□h

# Chapter 24

We are nearing the end of Crystal. I thank you all for reading and voting and commenting. I love you all to the moon and back.

I am shopping for new ideas for another book if you have any suggestions I am open......

Again thank you for reading and showing love..

xoxox.....

Constance dismissed the lady's maid from her room. She needed to think. This was the day she would finally be free, she would be free from William and maybe start her own life. She had caused so much grief all in aid of nothing. She had never meant for her father to pass on. She would become the Duchess and bring them to live with her, that was her plan when she met William, he was not supposed to die. She had written a letter to her mother but had not received a reply. In her heart she hoped it was because of a delay in receiving it. She hoped and prayed. If her mother too was gone she truly had no one. Wickam was her brother but he had his own family and his own responsibilities. When he married Sarah, as everyone knew he would, she did not expect her to take her into their home. She was the woman who had ruined the reputation of her sister.

There would be no love among them. But today she would be free to live as she pleased. She stood up and looked at her reflection, her dress was crimson so was the color on her lips. Her hair was held up with two loose strands on either side, dangling but barely touching her neck. She smoothed her gown before picking her hat and leaving the room. It was night to be prepared for, this was her final show.

Wickam straightened his tie. He and Constance had corresponded with each other since their meeting. He had gone to London and spent an entire day with her, they had talked and he had told her of family, his mother was very eager to meet her. He was raised in household of boys and never knew the light touch of a sister. She had told him of her life, he had look she about him, she always received looks when she spoke of what befell her sister, only Wickam did not give her a look of contempt that always followed. He only nodded in understanding of her choices. He too had once wanted to be like the men in the army. Moving from one village to another leaving children every place when his best friend had died.

It was a moment of awakening for him, he had no children and no wife, he would be mourned only by his family and his brothers in war but there was no woman who would grieve him. There was no one who would remember him for the man that he was, the provider, the friend, the lover. He had wanted to leave a heart so broken it could never heal. But he realized his reasoning was selfish, if he wanted a wife, he would wait until he finished his duties to his country then he would marry. He would leave a woman destitute, not after his mother had told him of his father's story. He did not want another man raising his own flesh and blood.

It was this thought that caused an awakening in him and he was thankful, for now he had found a woman worthy of love. She was a little extra than what he imagined his wife to be but she was truly perfect. Her opinions and thoughts and her bursts of energy gave him life. They gave him reason to smile. Lady Sarah Weldrake, after this ordeal was over he would ask for her hand in marriage like the honorable man he was. He only hoped she would permit Constance to live with them. He did not want to watch his family die alone. She did not want to die alone.

**

Jane put no effort in her dressing, she was tired and did not want to attend this ball. Why her father was throwing one was beyond her. It was much later in the year and the seasons were over, the weather was turning for the worst, why would he want people travelling in the rains? Their carriages would not doubt be stuck all along the roads. If they did happen to arrive it would be a fuss about the house which was, in her opinion, not in the least bit necessary. He had said it was to celebrate her coming wedding, but there was nothing to celebrate. Sarah had given up nursing her feelings and now only told her the truth of the matter, she would not be accepted back into society. There were many occasions that required the presence of young ladies like herself but they had received no invitation. Even though she was not with child, the women did not want their daughters in her company. She dallied with men of no class, and William of course was now regarded among his peers as a real man for still having a woman smitten over him even though he made promises to another.

Jane did not care for any of that, she had been happy in her solitude. She and Derek had found each other's company satisfying, but now he was making a life for himself. He and Lady Maria spent every waking moment in each other's company and when he was not with her he was speaking of her. Jane was happy for him. She was happy for Sarah too.

She had contemplated moving to Bath, it was much quieter and that is where all the spinsters retired to once they saw no proposal in sight. It would be a beautiful life, no hurt for there were hardly any men in Bath and if you had the unfortunate pleasure to find one he was far too old or fat or not with any agreeable manner about him. She could be happy there, she could heal and never feel the way she felt now. A knock on the door drew her from her thoughts. Derek opened the door not waiting for her to inquire who it was, in tow was Maria.

'Jane you are not ready.'

'Of course I am.'

He looked her over she was draped in what looked like a sheet, her hair was in a loose braid and looked very unkempt. There was no color on her face whatsoever and the slippers on her feet were less than presentable. She looked like a housemaid only without the ever present color of soot etched across her face. 'This cannot do Jane, you look terrible.'

'I am in no mood to attend I told papa and I will tell you the same. If am to be forced downstairs I will go looking the way I want. If William feels I am far too plain or ugly then it will settle this matter, I will retire to Bath and the family can continue on in happiness without the memory of shame I have brought upon us.'

'If I believed in raising my hand to a woman I would do it. Do not speak such nonsense Jane. You have brought no shame here.'

'Sarah has been cast from the very people that she used to gossip about others with. They are now sharing gossip about her. It is my fault she has now been cast out from the bossom of society. If Wickam does not propose no mother in their right mind will let their sons near any female in this family. Mama and papa will be invited only because he is a Duke, but even when they attend balls and papa goes to the courts people will talk.'

'You have always been smarter than the rest of us, this level of stupidity I can only blame on William,' he remarked. Jane had lost all the confidence in her own choices. She was now like the rest of the women thinking only of what they had done to deserve the hand that was being dealt to them.

'It is not stupidity Derek, it is sense and circumstance.'

'Is this because Matthew has refused to entertain you?' Jane remained silent, 'it is, isn't it. He is one man. If he has not heard by now we can blame it on his lack of better judgment. They set the very rumor concerning a child straight. He must be nursing a bruised ego that is the reason we have not seen him. What if he is attendance tonight?'

'He would not show his face here. He hates me.'

'You do not believe in yourself enough Janie.'

Maria maintained her position behind Derek as she watched the two siblings go at each other. Jane was firm in her decisions. Maria doubted they would see her tonight. She too was kept in the dark on the agenda for the evening, but Derek had promised her entertainment beyond anything she had ever seen. She saw the look in Jane's eyes and knew she was a woman bleeding on the inside and nothing her brother said to her would change her mind or give her hope to think otherwise. She placed her hand on Derek's when he began to speak again, 'let me talk to her,' she whispered to him. 'Woman to woman, I may have more impact than your masculine chauvinistic ways of reasoning.' Derek ignored the comment and stepped aside. 'In private,' she added.

He glared at Jane, his anger rising. His sister would not rot away he had seen to it. It had taken their father much convincing to do what they were about to do tonight and here she was drowning herself in self pity. This was not the woman he had grown with. He left and closed the door, but remained close enough to usher her downstairs when she finally emerged.

'Forgive my forwardness, Lady Jane.'

'Please, at this moment whatever station you hold, you are far higher than I, call me Jane.'

'I will call you so only because I predict we shall soon be sisters and not for any other reason. You look malnourished, have you not been eating?'

'How can one eat in my situation?'

Maria led her to the mirror and sat her down, she began undoing the braid and brushing her hair, 'It is not all that bad. My father ran us into the ground. He had a bad gambling habit. The only time my mother gave him compliments was when he would have the luck to win a hand and he came home with a gem stone for her.'

'I am sorry,' Jane was now more interested in what Maria was saying than what she was doing. She met her eyes in the mirror and she saw the pain behind them.

'It's not you doing. The life we live now, we can barely afford. My mother has pushed me into the arms of every man from Italy to England, hoping I will find a match, a wealthy match, that will take care of her. I never had what you had, a family that cares for me. My sole purpose in life is to marry and create wealth for my mother.'

'Is that why you have set your sights on Derek?'

Maria laughed. He was right, Jane would do anything for her family and she would use this to make her presentable for the evening's festivities. 'No, I can assure you that. When I met you both in London I was convinced you were his fiancée, but I spoke to him anyway. I found him quite agreeable. He was funny and still is and he loves you and Sarah ever so greatly. A man who can love his family the way he loves you is a man who can love his wife.'

'What do you mean by that?'

'Derek said you were too smart for me. I have been caught I am afraid, but I beg you to act surprised. He went through all this to announce our engagement. He assumed it would be enough reason to remove you from this room and put a smile on your face.'

Jane smiled, her biggest smile in a long time. 'Oh now that is good news, splendid. Does papa know?'

'No, we want to announce to everyone including your family all together.'

'And you mother, she must be glad you have found a man who loves you.'

'My mother will not be attending,' he tone changed. She had thought about the moment she would find a man who would want to marry her. When the day came would she invite her mother? She had done nothing but patronize her and push her and tell her she was not good enough or beautiful enough to secure a man of any good social standing. She had talked of all the things she would do when Maria got married. She would travel the world, go to Spain, maybe Italy or France. Did Maria want to live under the shadow of her mother all her life, even when she had settled in her own home?

'She is your mother.'

'She is a woman who brought me into this world and that is all she did. She did not raise me in any way. I had to teach myself and life gave me a few more lessons.

Jane put her hand on Maria's and met her eyes in the mirror.

'Let me finish making you beautiful. Your brother will want you to be by his side.'

JPNYD

# Chapter 25

----------------------------------------------------------------

We have a one more stretch to go.....

Thanks for reading..

xoxox....

Maria left Jane's room feeling proud of herself for having convinced her to join the party, but she also felt guilty for telling her a lie. She knew Jane was a calm lady by description but she heard from Derek his sister was not the most forgiving being in the world. She took trust and loyalty very seriously. Maria stayed confident in Derek's words, once she found out why they had done what they did she would understand, she hoped.

She had left her future family member to put on her dress with the help of a lady's maid. She had made her hair and added colour to her face. Jane was beautiful and she was grateful she was Derek's sister, for if she too would be vying for his hand she would not stand a chance against her. Which made her question why so many had turned away from her when she had her first season. Surely she, much younger then, had the gift of youth and beauty, then why did they not fall over each other for her hand.

'There you are, is Jane ready?' Derek said as he was walking up the stairs. Maria simply nodded. 'What is the matter?' his eyes so blue looked into hers with concern. She saw this man before her, he was beautiful and he had a beautiful soul. She knew she was being a silly girl but the lie she had told Jane was what her heart truly desired. She knew Derek did not care for title or prestige but his father would. He would never let his son marry into a family of bankruptcy and gambling. Her mother was widely known for her less than discreet escapades and she did not try to hide her love and want for money and prestige. No doubt the Duke knew of her and even though she had been welcomed into their home she had often seen the look on the Duke's face, it was less than pleasing. She often wondered what his father thought of her. She knew she was nothing like her mother but she did not expect the rest of the world to know that. The English society was a cruel one and they judged every chance they got.

'Nothing is the matter, I feel for Jane. She is clearly heartbroken and she will hate both you and me tonight.'

He reached her and took her hands, Derek had been around women to know that is not what was bothering her but he responded to her anyway, 'She will not hate us, she will be upset for a while but grateful at the end of it all.'

'You are her family she has no choice but to forgive you, your father will order it.'

He laughed, 'What's the matter Maria. I know my sister's troubles are barely affecting your heart. Tell me,' he said while leading her down the stairs. One thing Derek was forever grateful to his father for was the liberties they were afforded within their household. He believed in his ability to raise upright children and even though at times they would step out of line, they never really caused any damage. In another household, it would be a grand taboo for him to be walking hand in hand with a woman he had not already spoken for.

'You have a beautiful family and I am envious, that is all. I never had a sister to talk to or a mother who would go through lengths such as these for me. My mother is a whore and all of England knows this.'

'And you are worried her choices in life will sway the opinion of you in the face of my father?'

Maria stopped walking. 'It is written all over your face and Jane mentioned as much to me. You have nothing to worry about. If my father did not want you here, you would not have made it past the first luncheon. My first attachment was sent fleeing from this very house,' he smiled trying to ease her mood but it only made her return a small smile in return. 'Maria, I have chosen you and if you think I have not asked for your hand yet because I am afraid of what may come of it I can assure you the only reason I haven't asked for your hand is because as Jane's elder brother I must make sure she is safe and secure before I can think of my own happiness. Imagine me laying awake at night with you, my wife, beside me and my sister has retired to an old maid's home. It wouldn't be right and Wickam asked for our help tonight. We can offer it and after all this is done you and I will speak to my father and I will offer for your hand then.'

Maria smiled, how had the Duke and Duchess managed to raise such well mannered children? She hoped she would one day be a good a mother to her children, if she was destined to have any.

'Come, Jane is ready and there are things you and I need to prepare. This is after all going to be a beautiful night.' He hoped he had put her fears and worries to rest. Jane seemed to like her a great deal more than he liked Leila, and Jane had always been an excellent judge of character. He led her down the stairs to the drawing room and closed the door behind them.

**

The night was still young but the energy was the highest it had ever been guests had begun their arrival, carriages bearing every symbol stopped in front of the Devonshire manor doors. Rich women and their husbands descended dressed like they were attending a palace ball. Jane was at her window watching as the guests arrived, she did not know why a thing such as engagement brought the best of the ton all the way to Devonshire. She saw two carriages with symbols she did not even recognize. She assumed they belonged to a family new to the elite society. Oh how they would be disappointed this life may be full of wealth and prestige but it was very lonely and it was full of disappointments and heartaches. She was lost in thought when the sound of a particular carriage brought her back to her reality.

There he was, she was a landing above them but she'd recognize that frame anywhere from any height. It was Matthew. He stood at the door of the carriage traveling the walls with his eyes. They climbed the vines and landed on her window. Jane felt her heart skip a beat, for a moment their eyes locked on each other before she jumped out of eyesight. Her whole body began shaking. What on earth was he doing here? Did Derek not know he was the last man she wanted to see? Yes, she was Charlotte's bother but Charlotte had been under lock and key and she doubted her mother would release her unless the King himself ordered it and even then she was not sure.

She approached the window again and to her disappointment he was still there, his eyes had found something else of fascination to focus on but he was still there. She could see him plain as day. Why had he come? Had Derek invited him? Her brother would hear from her when this night was over. He had no right inviting Matthew here. She watched from behind the veil of the curtain. He had extended his hand for someone in the carriage, Jane was sure it would be his sister she would soon see, but her heart stopped. The woman that appeared had chestnut hair straight as any she had ever seen. It was not very "ton" to have your hair that straight and even more scandalous it was flowing down her back. She tossed her head to the side as she laughed at something Matthew had said. How dare he! She stomped her foot and regretted it immediately as pain shot through her leg.

Not waiting for the pain to subside she looked back out the window, the carriage had disappeared but not Matthew, he was still standing there arm in arm with that woman. She hated herself more than ever. She had been too foolish to realize her feelings for the man and now here she was spying on him and raising a temper because he had found companionship in another woman. She did not expect him to move on ever so quickly as if she never existed. As if he had never wanted her for himself. Yes, she had been a little hasty in her affections for William, she was simply fascinated by his interest in her. She had had many seasons all fruitless save for the one time. But she was giving up and here comes a man who was willing to marry her. How wrong she had been.

She looked back out the window and he was gone. There was no Matthew and there was no woman. The next carriage that pulled up bore no symbols or emblems it was just a carriage. The footman approached it to open the door but it sprung open on its own and Constance took the three steps like a professional, like a woman who had had one too many unaccompanied carriage rides. Jane swallowed, Derek had a rather strange crowd arriving for his engagement. She was starting to think this was no engagement party. There was something else going on here. Constance did not continue forward, instead she reached back into the carriage and out came a little boy no older than five. He had similar hair to Constance, a full head of it. She had never seen children that young at any gathering, she always thought it was forbidden. She tried to lean hard against the glass hoping to get a better look at the boy as he looked around in awe of his surroundings. He looked like someone who had never seen a house this big. It never amazed Jane, only when they were at the King's palace. She took hold of his hand and led him down the stone path instead of through the door everyone else was using.

The door opened and Jane jumped back from the window. She did not want anyone to know she had seen half the guests arrive, the only one she had not yet spotted was William. 'What on earth are you doing by that window Janie?' Sarah asked.

'I was looking at the guests arriving.'

'Anyone interesting, papa and Derek will not let me within earshot of any conversation they are having. I'm sure if you weren't locked up in here they would have told you and you would have told me. I do not like surprises.' Sarah knew her one advantage over Jane was her love for gossip. If she seemed like she did not know what was going on and was in desperate need of some information Jane would not think she too was involved in the happenings of the night.

'A few ton members that is all. You look lovely,' Jane said to change the subject. She was a bad liar and if her sister continued on that conversation she would revel all the people she saw arriving.

'Thank you,' Sarah said curtly. Her dress was a soft pink, it gathered at the waist then let loose all around her. Her bossom was perfectly framed in the dress and she was sparkling all over her chest. Her hair looked like a Greek goddess's, crown with lavender flowers woven through it. There were a few loose curls that gave her the seductive advantage. The men tonight would stand no chance against Sarah. Maria made my hair. Can you imagine when she is our sister, we will be the most beautiful girls at the balls. Our husbands of course dripping with jealousy over all the attention we shall be getting from other men. It will be such a scandal.'

'We are not yet married Sarah.'

'But we all shall be soon,' she winked. 'Mama asked me to come and get you. She wants you, Derek and I to walk down with them.' She looked Jane over and smiled, William was in for the surprise of his life and Matthew was about to be the happiest man alive.

**

Their parents were waiting for them at the top of the staircase, Derek looked quite the sight in his black tailcoat and crisp white shirt. His trousers did his long and masculine legs justice as they showed every curve of his muscle and revealed the strength lying underneath. His hair was slicked back, unlike his usual nonchalant breezy hair. He was clean shaven and smelt lovely. His eyes, blue like hers, stood out today and the twinkling in them told her this was not a simple engagement. Derek was not one to celebrate an accomplishment of his own life. She took his arm as Sarah placed herself on his left side and they walked down slowly.

'You are the sight to behold tonight. You have stolen the show from me and my fiancée I dare say,' he whispered into Jane's ear. She made no acknowledgment of his comment. Her thoughts were too focused on eyeing the crowd. Half of them were present when William's damned woman friend had made them all believe she was with child. And now here they all were, their faces turned when they were announced the room fell into a silence then soft murmurs began from the centre of the room and spread. By the time they reached the bottom the whole room was buzzing with silent voices. Jane wanted to turn round and return to the safety behind her closed doors. She should never have let Maria talk her into coming down here. Derek sensing her fear dropped Sarah's hand and turned to face Jane. His eyes said it all. He would be there for her if she felt like it was all too much for her. To her surprise Sarah placed herself by her side and whispered comforting words into her ear.

Jane took a tighter hold of Derek's hand when she felt him release her. 'Jane, I cannot stand by your side the whole evening.'

'Yes, you can,' she whispered. 'I did not want to come down here'

'Janie, let go,' he said between gritted teeth. He smiled at an approaching couple. 'We have company.'

The man and woman stopped just in front of them and gave their greetings. Jane recognized them, 'My dear Lady Jane,' you look splendid tonight. You must be beside yourself with excitement. William is to take you this very night. You and your child will be in safe hands, I am sure,' the woman said her last words coated in sarcasm. She bowed and promptly left dragging her husband with her.

'This is not where I want to be Derek please tell mama and papa I am very sorry,' with that she let go of Derek's hand and ran up the stairs making sure not to fall over her dress. She reached the top and made for her famous plant that provided her with the cover she needed when she wanted to watch the dancing of the night.

The music played on and on and people danced and talked and had their feel of the fine assortments that were put out on display. She heard a few women commenting on the extreme tenderness of the cakes and the bitterness of the wine. This society always had one thing or another to complain about. Then her eyes caught him, it was Matthew with that damned woman. They were enjoying the waltz. He was turning her around and she laughed as her hair flew around her and landed neatly over her shoulder. She felt jealousy flow through her, she felt like marching down and putting that woman in her place. But she was no one to Matthew not even a friend. The only thing she could do now was watch as he turned his new dance and life partner. They swirled and his eyes ran across the room before landing back on his partner. He seemed to say something to her which made her laugh and tilt her head back.

Jane realized if she did not do something now she would surely loose the only man she has ever loved. She may start a scandal but it was better than living with a man you did not love. 'Jane,' a deep voice startled her. She jumped with her hand to her chest.

'William, what on earth? How did you get up here? When did you arrive?'

'That was not the response I got when we first met,' he smiled. He was dressed like her brother, in black, except his shirt was black too. He looked like a shadow, a dark shadow. His hair was combed well but it did not stay in place. When he took a step forward a strand fell out of place and onto his forehead. 'I was hoping to recreate the night we met, a touch of romance, don't you think?

'I think not William. I did not see you arrive,' she replied coldly

'I am of the impression you hate me.'

'I do not particularly like you at this moment.'

'And why is that?' he took a step forward

'Your lady friend is here. She is in the company of a young gentleman.'

'I do not care what Constance does with her time as I have already explained to you. She was simply deluded and was of the impression she and I were on a road to marriage. A delusion I set right and that is where all her madness is drawn from. If she has found herself another poor old sap to enchant well then, poor fellow,' he was not interested in talking about Constance. He was quite relieved when Jane mentioned the presence of another gentleman. It was better for her to come to terms with the fact she would never be the Duchess.

Jane knew he had misunderstood her but she did not care, she noticed him getting closer. She looked back to the floor, the song was soon coming to an end, she needed to speak with Matthew. She moved quickly around William. 'I apologize but there is someone I must speak to before it gets too late.' She rushed to the stairs hoping William was not behind her. She went down the stairs two at a time, twice almost falling. She did not fancy rolling down the stair case, her father would have a heart attack.

She reached the bottom as the music concluded and she landed in the hands of Constance. 'Lady Jane, if you may follow me, I wish to apologize for the agony I have recently caused you.'

Jane trying to walk past her but Constance made it impossible. She tried to look through the holes the bodies made in the crowd and find Matthew, but she could not make out where he had gone too. 'Lady Jane, please,' this time she offered her hand.

'Jane will be going nowhere with you,' William towered over both women as he placed himself between Constance and Jane.

'Always the one to speak for a woman,' Constance had seen him follow Jane up, she sent Matthew to dance with his lady friend, she was sure Jane would see them, she did not however know whether Jane would come down to try to speak with Matthew. Now that she had she knew William would not be far behind when he saw Constance approach her, that was exactly what she was hoping for.

'I am not sure how you wormed your way here Constance but you will stop the damage you seem so set on causing, not in this family, not in my family,' he had lowered his voice and not wanting to draw attention to them but Constance let out a shrilly laughter that cased everyone to turn. The music was long gone and the band did not look like they had another song to play they all set their instruments but kept their seats.

Jane wished the ground could open up and swallow her. She was morti-fied, this was happening to her again. Trouble seemed to follow William wherever he went. It was beyond her why this woman was so set on making sure he paid for not loving her. Women did not go to such lengths for men, even the loose ones knew when to give up, but Constance was not one of them. Matthew and Derek appeared from nowhere and suddenly Jane was trapped in a bubble of bodies. Wickam was on the platform clearing his voice as if prepared to make a speech, it was then Jane realized what this was. It was not an engagement party for her brother, but it was an intervention for William. Would he have to face his fears before wedding her, it must have been a condition her father had set. It was a shame she was not set out to marry the man she truly loved. She did not want to spend the rest of her life fending off this woman.

# Epilogue

The room stilled, every moving body stopped and turned like a wave. Jane was still a speck in the circle that had formed around her. Matthew was to her left and Derek to her right. Wickam looked over the crowd as if to check whether all the attention was on him. Jane looked to her left and found Matthew's eyes hard on her. She felt as if he was looking into her soul. She tried to speak but he shook his head and mouthed her a 'sssh' to indicate she should be silent. Constance was long gone, she had disappeared when Wickam cleared his throat. Jane was far too occupied trying to breathe evenly in the presence of Matthew, she wondered where his lady friend had disappeared to and why he had agreed to be party to this madness. She craned her neck trying to get a view of what was happening, she spotted Maria not too far away from them, she was beaming. She looked far happier than anyone else in the room.

Wickam's voice cut through her thoughts and turned her attention to him, she could only see his head but it would have to do because no one seemed to want to move. As he began to speak, Derek moved closer to her as did Matthew, cutting off direct contact between her and William. He now looked like he had never been close to her.

'Good evening Ladies and Gentlemen, I apologize for this interruption but fear not we shall be back to the festivities as soon as possible, there is a matter we wish to clarify first. My name is Wickam, many of you know me as the Second Lieutenant in the army. I have been residing with the Duke and Duchess Weldrake and their family, they have been nothing but hospitable to me and it is my duty to show the same kindness they have shown me,' he paused as he motioned to someone to join him on stage. Jane tried to get a better view but her brother kept her rooted to the ground, she could only make out the hair of a woman.

'This is my sister Constance, you may all remember her as the woman that set about the speculation of young Lady Weldrake being with child,' the room began to come alive again as women turned to each other, either reminding the other of the occurrence or relaying a story about the woman they had heard about the streets. 'She is truly sorry for what she has caused this family but she did not do it out of malice or ill intent, she was simply trying to defend her own.'

William watched as Wickam and Constance stood on the stage, he felt sorry for her, she had now chosen to side with a man claiming to be her brother. Her naivety was going to be her downfall. She trusted too easily and that was the one thing men took advantage of. He had asked around town and no one knew of Wickam's family. He was clearly a con and Constance was going to suffer for it. It mattered not him, however, the more attention she paid to this man the less attentions she was offering him. He was pleased Jane would see the last attempt by her to ruin him and she would get over the foolish notion that he and Constance had a past.

'Lady Constance Cartwright, future Duchess of Sussex, as she should be referred to, is the wife to Lord William Cedric Cartwright future Duke of Sussex.' This caused a gasp from the crowd and Jane as well. She turned to her brother who seemed far too calm, it could only mean... he knew. 'What on earth is going on here Derek?' she asked not waiting for an answer from him she turned to Matthew who only offered her silence.

So this why he had come to, watch her be humiliated in front of everyone. She took a step back and Derek did not try to stop her. He knew she was now angry but she would have to stay and listen to the rest of Wickam's speech. He hoped Sarah would play her part well and speak reason into Jane when all of this was over for he knew he would be the last person she wanted to see.

'Lord William married her and promised her a life together once he set his affairs in order and that was the last she saw of him. He would send her provisions for her up keep but made his presence extremely scarce,' the crowd gasped again and turned to William. He was red. All he wanted was to remove Constance and her false relation and give them a good lesson. All the women had now turned to him but the men kept their focus on Wickam. The judgment in their eyes told William if he did not do something he would soil his name and the name of his family and for that his father would never forgive him. Jasper had declined the invitation so had his parents and sister, he was grateful for that. If they were here his father would have speared him by now. He had to find away to stop this impossible charade. No one would believe her, it would be her word against his and he was more superior.

'Constance had the good fortune to sire a child with William,' Wickam continued and William's mouth dropped. He turned back to look at Jane but all he met were the warning eyes of her brother and Matthew. 'William steadily asked her to rid herself of any evidence he had ever been attached to her and simply disappeared, only sending enough to keep her fed. Constance had to turn to unruly and unladylike behavior to support herself and her unborn child.' The women began their conversations and throwing dangerous looks at William. He looked at the crowd before him and decided it was time for him to leave. He would deal with this another day. As he began to move a hand caught him. He turned round to look into the burning eyes of the Duke, 'Are you leaving so soon? The party has just begun,' he smiled.

William freed himself and stood his ground. He did not expect people to believe this foolish story, it would serve as good enough gossip until the next scandal.

'Constance, being madly in love with the man did the only thing she knew would bring back the William into her life. It is hard for a woman to do the unimaginable,' he paused when Constance put her hand on his arm. She was close to tears. She whispered something into Wickam's ear and he took a step back.

She was a brave woman to face the crowd the way she did knowing her word could easily be declared that of a disgruntled woman, her trying to shame William was a social death sentence, one she was very willing to take. 'I was asked to rid myself of any evidence William and I were married. I, to this day, cannot find the priest that married us and his best friend was our witness. I was alone in this world, my only strength was the child that was growing inside of me. I had left my family, my father died and I have not heard from my mother. He met them once and said they were not the kind of people he wished to associate himself with. I stopped communicating with my family for that man,' she pointed in William's direction.

Jane was still immersed in her shield of bodies, but heard every word. Was this the same man she had once envisioned a life with? He was capable of pulling a child from her family. Constance looked no older than she, she must have been but one and six when she met William. He had destroyed her life. Matthew had now moved closer to her and taken over the role Derek had previously played of making sure she does not run. It was a rather unfortunate evening, they had prepared an ambush for William and he was none the wiser. He looked shocked with every word that came from the podium and he looked like he was waiting for the final blow, the final nail to his coffin.

'I did not have the strength to do what he wanted me to do. My father was not a rich man but he provided for us, my sister and I. He and my mother would sleep hungry so we could eat. He could have easily chosen to be rid of us and live only with my mother but he did not. Who was I to kill an innocent child that had wronged no one. Will,' she turned around and held out her hand. A little boy came walking towards her and placed himself safely by her side, making sure to hide under the cover her gown. He looked afraid of the mass of people, 'This is my son, William II.'

Murmurs grew louder and louder and more and more eyes turned to William. 'ENOUGH!' he yelled. 'Are you all going to believe this mad woman. She is disgruntled. She forced herself into my bed. I am sure many of you in this room have had a taste of her. It is no secret my...' he stopped.

'Your what William?' Jane emerged. 'Your wife? Is that what you were going to say. How could you possibly ask a woman what you asked of Constance? Have you no heart?'

'That child could very well be your fathers,' William snapped. 'How do you think she was able to gain entrance the first time and she keeps coming back. Who is to say she is not having her way with him.'

'You will respect the Duke,' Wickam's voice thundered. 'In his home you will speak with only respect.'

'You are a fool,' he turned his rage to Wickam. 'You believe the pitiful story this harlot has brought you. Are you even her relation?'

'He has proven he is William. As always you are turning to tarnishing others instead of confessing to your sins.'

'What sins Constance? We were never truly married. The man who wed us was not a priest. He was a peasant I paid a good sum to make you believe we were. I needed pure blood to carry on my father's legacy not the tainted popper blood you carry.'

'William,' Jane gasped. What was this man? He seemed so gentle and caring yet the words coming out of his out at this time were of pure hatred and disgust. 'What is the matter with you?'

'Do not waste your breath Jane,' Constance spoke. 'This is William. He was never a gentleman. He has the powers of deceit, I too was fooled.' Her son pulled on her gown, she looked down and patted his head. 'I only wanted to set things right with you Jane and stop you from making the same mistake I did all those years ago.'

'Show that boy you claim is mine Constance, I ensure you there is no resemblance,' he spoke to the crowd. 'It would not surprise me if the boy resembled another man in this room.'

Constance knelt until she was at eye level with boy, she whispered something in his ear and he nodded. He took a step away from her and it was clear, there was no room for denying it. The boy looked exactly like William, except for his eyes, they held his mother's mystery. He had the same hair, the same nose, the shape of his lip was a match, even William stood perfectly still. There was no denying the boy was his. 'What type of sorcery is this?'

'It is no sorcery William. This is what you asked me to give up. How selfish could you have been to deny me the joy of being a mother simply because you did not want to be accountable to me? Is your heart that wicked?'

'It is clear,' Wickam spoke. 'We spoke with your father yesterday William. He did not entertain the idea of his grandson being raised by myself and my sister. He has offered shelter for Constance and her son, your son. He also insisted a marriage be carried out in a fortnight so as to raise the boy in a complete family.'

'That is nonsense!'

'William, your days of deceit are over.'

'He does not have to marry me,' Constance cut him off. 'All I want is he be a father to his son and provide love and care.'

William stormed out pushing anyone in his way. He left a trail of grumbles in his wake. Once he had exited, the whole room began to give applause, Jane thought she heard a few women say they thanked Constance for finally putting him in his place. She was baffled at what she had just witnessed. Constance and Wickam left the podium with little William and made their way to her. The boy was a handsome young man. She hoped he would not grow to be like his father,.

'I wish to apologize to you Jane. I meant you no harm. When I first arrived I was prepared to do away with because I was under the impression William was giving what he had promised me to another. Once news of my father's passing came to me I realized I had spent too many years being spiteful for this man. It was no longer worth the price I was paying.'

'Your boy is lovely,' she spoke while keeping her eyes on him. He smiled for an instant then disappeared behind her gown.

'It may be much to ask but I would be grateful to hear the words I forgive you. It will put my heart at ease.

'You expect too much Constance.'

'I know, but I know what it feels like to be ever so desperately in love but I also know what it feels like to hurt. And I hurt, William took everything I had, I did not wish the same for you.'

'You have your title, is that not what you were after?'

'I declined the Duke's offer. I am not interested in being married to that man. I fear he would one day kill me for the shame and embarrassment I caused him.'

'How were you able to hide a child?'

'It was rather simple I did not leave my home until he was born. It was a lonely life and I am thankful to be rid of it.'

'I am afraid forgiveness is not something I can offer you now Constance, I do not hate you but you are not particularly in my good graces. You cost me a friendship and a love that I held very dear to me. You ruined my life. Do not expect me to owe you anything because you exposed William.'

'I understand. I only hope one day we may look back to this day and laugh over it.' she excused herself and William.

**

It had been a long evening and fatigue washed over her. She only wanted to lock herself away and thank God he had saved her from a disastrous marriage but mourn over Matthew, she had lost him. He must have known and came with company to cover him for the night. Jane felt her heart tear into pieces as she watched Constance walk away. Maria and Derek were whispering to each other, they looked happier than ever. Jane tried to find Sarah but she knew she must have gone after Wickam. She turned to go back to solitude but she was now face to face with Matthew. The pity in his eyes broke her heart. He felt sorry for her. She much preferred hatred to pity. She knew she would not sleep this night. It had been far too long and far too painful.

'How are you Jane?'

'As well as I can ever be. I suppose you could say there is a part of me that is thankful tonight happened. Now I do not have to chain myself to William.'

'Is that not what you wanted?'

'There was time it was...' her words trailed off and she was overcome by tears.

'Is there somewhere we can talk in private?' he hesitated to comfort her for he knew if he touched her would not be in control of the situation. She nodded and led him to the balcony, it was a perfect place, there was a large plant that blocked a good portion of it and no one ever came out there, her mother was far too frightened of its dungeon like demeanor. 'It has been a rather eventful night and I am afraid it is about to become even more eventful for some of us.'

'I saw you arrive with your lady friend, Matthew. You do not owe me any explanations, I was to marry another man yet I carried affections for you.'

'Is that what you think? You think I would replace you?'

'I do not think it Matthew it has happened.'

'The lady I arrived with,' Matthew smiled, 'is a distant relative. Since Charlotte is not able to move about town as she once loved, mama asked me to chaperon her. Her season begins next year, she is but a child. Were you jealous?'

Jane was not able to process what he was saying.

'You look confused, what I am trying to say is this Janie,' he took her hands in his, 'I kissed you that day not on impulse but because I felt if I left without knowing what it felt like you would never really know my true feelings. I want you and only you. Yes I was upset you chose to marry William, it was only fair you knew him first I was a stranger that crept upon you and invaded your privacy,' she tried to speak but he shook his head. 'You do not have to explain. I was of the opinion since you and William are no longer attached you and I may form our own attachment. Your mother would be glad. Three proposals in one evening. Your family has fortune Jane.'

'Three?'

'Will you do me the honor of marrying me Lady Jane Weldrake.'

She was overcome with joy. Never did she imagine she would be this happy. She had been on the marriage mart for four years and had given up. She was never as beautiful as the other girls and yet here she was on a balcony with a man who was pure in his love asking for her hand. Where had she gotten such luck?

'Jane, I expect an answer or I shall spend the rest of my days sulking.'

'Of course I will marry you. I was sure you would never ask.'

Matthew smiled, here was the Jane knew. 'That is not the way women are meant to answer that question wife.'

'I am not your wife yet Lord Matthew, I suggest we do not get ahead of ourselves.'

He pulled her close and kissed her, and just like the first time it was beautiful. They both got lost in each other, forgetting the room filled with people or the shock they had encountered only moments before. Jane was happy, she had lost her heart to a fool in the past and almost made the same mistake again. Matthew had saved her and now he was everything she wanted and hoped for. She had prayed and asked for a man that knew her soul and loved it and here he was. God has answered her prayers. When they finally came up for air, Jane was smiling, her heart was overwhelmed with joy, but there was something that Matthew had said she had not quite understood.

'You said we would have three engagements...' her words were drowned out by the sound of cheers.

'Yes, I believe that is cheer for your sister and brother. Wickam will make an honest woman of Sarah.' He kissed her again, a gentle brush on her lips. He loved how she smelled of flowers and freshness. He would have all his life to know her, to know every inch of her. He would not leave anything to chance. She was his and his forever.

He pulled away from her knowing he would not be able to stop if they did not join the rest of the party, he had a lifetime for that and he did not want to compromise Jane anymore than she already had been.

'Let us go and make your mother proud,' he said as he took her hand and led her inside.